"What do you think? Isn't she ideal for the job?"

Dani's face flushed under the scrutinizing gaze of both men. She felt like an inanimate object and she didn't like it one bit. "Well, if you care to let me in on your secret, maybe I can tell you if I'm right for the job."

"I'm sorry, Dani." Mark gave her a big smile. "You're the most important person in this project. Of course, you have to be sold on the idea, too."

Feeling her temper subside, Dani made an effort to respond calmly. "A new book?"

"Yes, and an explosive one, I think. At least if we can dig up the kind of information I'm hoping for." Mark sat at his desk, resting his chin on steepled fingers.

"You know how much pride we Americans take in our National Park System, and rightly so. But not much is known about the rangers—the inside story— what they do in their free time, how they spend their money."

Suddenly Dani felt soiled and apprehensive. What was he leading up to? Surely he wasn't planning an exposé on the men in green!

THROUGH THE VALLEY OF LOVE

Shirley Cook

Serenade/Serenata
BOOKS
of the Zondervan Publishing House
Grand Rapids, Michigan

A Note from the Author:
I love to hear from my readers! You may correspond with me by writing:

> Shirley Cook
> Author Relations
> 1415 Lake Drive, S.E.
> Grand Rapids, MI 49506

THROUGH THE VALLEY OF LOVE
Copyright © 1987 by Shirley Cook

Serenade/Serenata is an imprint of Zondervan Publishing House, 1415 Lake Drive, S.E., Grand Rapids, MI 49506.

ISBN 0-310-47382-9

Scripture quotations are taken from the *Holy Bible: New International Version* (North American Edition), copyright © 1973, 1978, 1984, by the International Bible Society, used by permission of Zondervan Bible Publishers; and the King James Version of the Bible.

Yosemite Valley Map, courtesy of the National Park Service.

Edited by Lynda S. Parrish
Designed by Kim Koning

Printed in the United States of America

87 88 89 90 91 92 / LP / 10 9 8 7 6 5 4 3 2 1

This book is dedicated to the men and women who serve as rangers in the National Park Service. It is because of their love and knowledge of the wilderness that we and our children can enjoy its beauty now and in the future. I especially thank park rangers at Yosemite Valley and Point Reyes for their patience in answering my many questions.

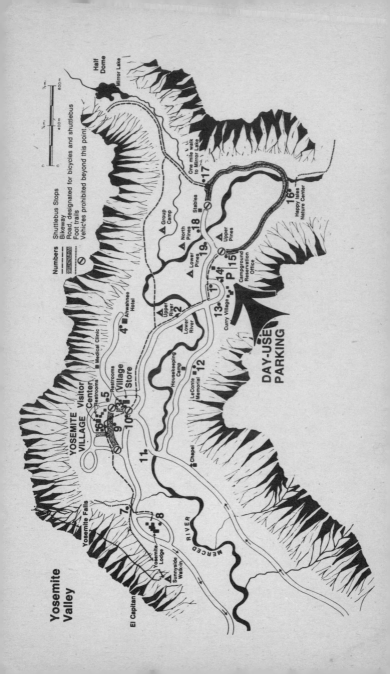

CHAPTER 1

"HEY, BOOKWORM, IF YOU CAN GET your nose out of that research for a few minutes, Mr. Hutchinson wants to see you in his office."

Danielle Fuller reluctantly looked up from the large volume on her desk to the smiling woman in front of her. "Oh, Claire, I can't stop now. I'm on the verge of tracing down that piece of land the government stole from Andrew Brown."

Dani stretched her arms over her head and glanced out the window at the San Francisco skyline. "How does Mark expect me to finish this project if I'm always interrupted?"

"Oh, so it's Mark now, huh?" The short middle-aged woman rolled her eyes and tipped her head to one side. "I wouldn't knock it, kiddo. I think he likes you a lot."

Pretending not to hear Claire's last remark, Dani shuffled papers and stacked them in a neat pile on the corner of her desk. It was true, though. Mark Hutchinson had been showing her more attention than usual lately, but then she had been working on a special job for his newest book. His interest in her was strictly business. She was certain of that.

With a quick look in the mirror she kept in her top desk drawer, Dani dabbed shiny gloss on already rosy lips and shoved long sunny hair behind her shoulders. Her blue eyes sparkled with excitement at being summoned into the private office of her employer. She must keep calm. He probably wanted to suggest additional research material. Nothing more.

Crossing the room of clattering typewriters and inquisitive eyes, Dani was glad she had worn her burgundy angora sweater today. She knew the color complemented her skin tones and drew attention to the gold highlights in her hair, and as a lowly research assistant, she wasn't often called to the front office.

Lifting her chin as she reached Claire's desk, she smiled down at the secretary only briefly before approaching the heavy oak door.

"Go on in," Claire said, a twinkle in her eyes. "He's waiting for you."

Mark Hutchinson, seated behind an oversized desk, rose to his feet as she entered, and from the corner of her eye, she noticed another man rise from the leather sofa at the side of the room. Both men appraised her with obvious admiration before Mark spoke. "Danielle Fuller, I'd like you to meet Ken Bridges."

Bridges, an overweight man in a crumpled suit, nodded briefly before slumping into a chair near the desk. Dani thought he looked out of place in the elegant surroundings, but before she could decide why, Mark had stepped quickly to her side and held out a chair for her.

"I think I have a proposition that will interest you, Miss Fuller."

As the handsome owner of Westcoast Publishing Company leaned against the edge of his desk, he do. But I promise you this, by the time we say good-night, you'll have my answer."

"That sounds like a challenge." Mark looked down on her with an intensity that sent a shiver through her body. "All I have to do is convince you that this assignment will benefit your career. Right?"

He rested his hand on her shoulder as she closed the door behind them.

"That's right, Mr. Hutchinson. I need to be convinced."

The drive through the city streets was quiet, except for the soft music filling the rich interior of the black Mercedes. Mark seemed lost in his own thoughts, and Dani used every opportunity to snatch glances at the handsome man. Several times, he caught her looking at him, and smiled broadly. "I'm not sure I'll let you go, Danielle Fuller."

When he pulled up in front of a small restaurant on a narrow side street, Dani felt disappointed. She had imagined dinner at the Hyatt Regency or the Fairmont on Nob Hill. However, as Mark opened the door to Pierre's her apprehensions faded. A balding man in a tuxedo greeted them. "Monsieur Hutchinson, how good to see you again." He bowed deeply over Dani's hand. "And Madamoiselle, my establishment is brighter because of your presence."

As Dani and Mark followed Pierre between tables in the dimly lit room, she did feel like Cinderella. They stopped at a small corner table draped in white lace and lit by one candle set in a crystal holder. A long-stemmed red rose had been laid beside her plate, and Dani glowed with pleasure. She would enjoy this fairy-tale evening to the fullest. It would only happen once, no matter what her decision. If she gave a no answer, Mark would pursue some other woman for the assignment, and if her answer was yes, she'd be heading for the mountains and campfires before the week was out.

CHAPTER 2

SIX DAYS HAD PASSED since that beautiful evening with Mark Hutchinson, and Dani was on her way. It had only taken a few days to pack her clothes, and the young woman across the hall had agreed to water her plants. Mark even assured her that he'd look in on her apartment from time to time. She would stay in Yosemite through the summer, returning to San Francisco at the end of August. During the busy tourist season, the rangers wouldn't notice one more person taking pictures and asking questions. The time, the setting, everything was perfect. Mark Hutchinson would surely have another bestseller to his credit.

Thinking about Mark brought a smile to Dani's face as she turned off Highway 99 at Merced for a cup of coffee. From there she would take 140 to Yosemite. Her trip had taken longer than usual, because she had spent the night in Lodi with her parents, nodding dutifully as they gave her instructions on how to make the most of this "wonderful opportunity." She hadn't told them the real purpose of her trip, only that she was to do some research on national parks.

"I'm so glad you're finally getting away from San Francisco," her father had said, blowing a breath of steam on his glasses. He polished them carefully with his handkerchief and mumbled under his heavy gray mustache, "Such an ungodly place."

She listened quietly as her mother admonished her to live for God, and try to find a nice young man to marry. "You should be settled down and raising a family by now." It was the same song—same verse. They didn't seem to realize that times had changed. Women had options other than housework and diapers. It was no use arguing though, so when she kissed them good-by this morning, it was with a heavy heart that they didn't understand her—or she them.

After a hurried stop at a coffee shop, Dani was again on the road—destination, Mariposa, a little town about forty miles from Yosemite. She dreaded it. Ken Bridges was to meet her there at the Waterwheel Café and give her papers of recommendation and other details of her new job. He was repulsive. His thin, greasy hair and pockmarked face made her shudder, and although she hadn't seen him since that Monday at the office, she still felt uneasy about him.

That Monday. Only six days ago. Much had happened since then. Mark had literally swept her off her feet when she told him of her decision to go to Yosemite. He had lifted her off the ground, whirled her around, then kissed her. She knew that to him it was only a spontaneous action, but throughout the rest of the evening, her lips burned from his kiss.

He ended their business date with only a handshake at the door. She was right. It was all business with him. Tying up a few details, making some phone calls, and sitting in on a conference with Mark was all that she needed to do before leaving. Joshua Talbott expected a companion for his mother immediately or he would make other arrangements. He sounded like a harsh man who very likely was hiding something, as Mark suspected.

The grassy foothills from Merced to Mariposa were electric green from the long, wet winter and spring. Wildflowers of every color bloomed profusely, and although the air was crisp and cool, Dani rolled down the window of her small Japanese car to let the wind whip through her hair. As she neared her destination, she could feel her heart pounding. What a change. From life in a busy metropolitan city to a remote mountain peak. What price glory. And it would be glory. She was determined to uncover as much information as possible to get at the truth.

More than anything, she wanted to prove to herself that just because she had been raised in a parsonage, she didn't have to settle down in the suburbs with a husband and children to be happy. She wanted excitement. Adventure. Yes, there was room in her life for romance, too, maybe even marriage someday, but for now . . .

Late afternoon sun slanted through the rear window of the car and warmed her back as she drove into Mariposa. The sign announcing a population of 1,017 brought a smile to her lips. What did people do for fun in a place like this? A white church with a cross on its steeple sat on a hill at the right of the road. Funny, she always noticed the churches in a town. Probably a leftover habit from childhood. The buildings were old, and the sidewalks rose about a foot from the street level.

Dani glanced at her dashboard clock. It was past four-thirty, and she was to meet Bridges at five. She drove to the motel where reservations had been made for her and left her suitcases in the small musty-smelling room. A quick comb through her hair, and she was ready to go again. No matter that her slacks were creased from sitting so long, or that her makeup had disappeared. She had no desire to freshen up for this dinner companion.

An involuntary shudder passed over her as she drove up to the café and stepped out of her car. The short, pudgy man stood outside, leaning against the fly-specked window, sucking on a soggy cigar.

"About time, baby." Bridges eyed her from head to toe. "You're late."

"It's only quarter after five—not that late," Dani snapped. She breezed ahead of Bridges and slid into a booth next to the window. Burying her face in the menu to keep from looking at the man across from her, she wondered if she'd made the right choice in coming.

"Let's get down to business," Ken leaned toward her, gray smoke circling his head and drifting into his squinty eyes. "Then we can get better acquainted. After all," he added with a wink, "we're going to be partners."

Dani felt a shock begin at the base of her spine and travel to the roots of her hair. "Mr. Bridges, we are not partners. I work for Mr. Hutchinson. You are a go-between, nothing more. My understanding is that the information I gather will be passed on to you in my way, and at my discretion." Dani folded her arms in front of her and glared at the man filling the opposite seat.

"Don't be so high and mighty," Bridges snarled. "We both work for Hutchinson, and my job is to pass on the filth you manage to scrape up." His eyes roamed slowly from her face to her shoulders, and she folded her arms tighter as a shield. "You put on an air of 'Miss Goody-Two-Shoes,' but you're no better than I am. And don't you forget it."

The waitress placed a greasy hamburger in front of

Dani and set a plate overflowing with some kind of brown meat smothered in pale gravy before Ken Bridges. Dani's stomach churned as he smacked his lips and scraped his plate clean. She felt sickened by her surroundings, yet even worse were the words that echoed in her mind—*Filth . . . no better than I am.*

He was right. She had sunk low to accept this position, but it was too late to back out now. She had given Mark her word, and he had given her reason to believe that what she was doing was for the good of the people. "They should know what these so-called 'servants of the wilderness' are really like," he had said.

After the waitress cleared the table, Dani toyed with her cup of coffee while Ken set out the plans for her arrival in Yosemite Valley.

"We're not interested in the old lady, and she won't give you any trouble. She's recovering from a minor heart attack, and . . . ," Ken added, spreading out a folded yellow page and hooking wire-rim glasses over his large ears, ". . . let's see, she's religious—goes to church, a widow with only the one son." Ken peered over the top of his glasses. "That's where you come in. This Joshua Talbott is a cool customer. We don't know much about him. So far, he seems on the up and up—a little too good, Mark thinks. Just recently took the position in Yosemite Valley. Came from Mt. Ranier National Park up in Washington."

"What am I supposed to look for? Does Mr. Hutchinson think he's doing something dishonest or what?" Dani reached into her purse for a pen and notebook. "Give me some idea of how to go about this. I've never been a spy, you know."

"I thought you were supposed to be such a crack researcher—'so enterprising,' as our boss said." The sneer in his voice twisted his lips. "He thought you'd have your own ideas about researching this story.

Maybe he should have picked someone with more experience—if you know what I mean."

Dani felt her cheeks glow and exploded, "Listen, Mr. Bridges, you stick to your job, and I'll stick to mine. When do we meet again?"

She was eager to get away from this man and this horrible place, although the smoke and grease didn't seem to phase Bridges.

"I'll be in touch," he drawled, sliding out of the booth and slouching over her. "If you don't hear from Mark, you'll hear from me. I'll set the time and place."

She noticed a brown stain on the front of his shirt where a button hung by a single thread. "Oh, by the way," he continued, "here's your letter of recommendation and a resume to be given to Talbott. It says here that you're an experienced nurse and have worked with geriatric patients for two years."

"Oh, great. Suppose Mrs. Talbott has another heart attack and I don't know what to do?"

"That's your problem, Goody-Two-Shoes. Just get your story."

With a sigh of relief, Dani watched the man lumber out the front door. She waited several minutes to be sure he was gone, then realizing he'd left her with the bill, she paid the waitress and stepped outside. The fresh mountain air cleared her head, and she walked briskly to her car, glad for a familiar haven in an unfamiliar world.

The drive to the motel led past a small frame church, its windows orange from the light within. She'd almost forgotten it was Sunday. She could hear strains of music drifting on the evening breezes, and lifted her foot off the accelerator as she coasted by.

"What a Friend We Have in Jesus" was a familiar hymn, and unconsciously she sang the words in her head, *All our sins and griefs to bear*. No. This was a new day . . . a new life for her. She still believed in God, but his restrictions were too narrow for the plans she had for her life. When she left home for college, she left her Christian walk behind. All her life, she had been tagged "Preacher's Kid" and because of that title, she never felt part of the "in" crowd. One day— maybe.

The crunch of gravel in the motel parking lot, the red neon sign flickering against the darkened sky, and the sounds of cars, not many now, passing through the small town, brought an unexpected yawn. Eight o'clock. By the time she had a shower and recorded her trip and meeting with Ken Bridges, she would be ready to fall into bed. She wanted to be at her best as she presented herself to Edna Talbott—and particularly to the mysterious chief ranger.

She smiled as she imagined a balding, craggy-faced man. What possible devious thing could he be up to? Mismanagement of park funds? Maybe. Political graft? Perhaps. An illicit love affair? Hardly. She'd have to wait and see. It was a good assignment, and regardless of Ken Bridges, she knew it could be exciting and fulfilling. She was doing it for herself, and she had to admit, she was also doing it for Mark Hutchinson. His suave ways and that one surprising kiss still burned in her memory.

After a good night's sleep and a light breakfast in a brightly clean coffee shop, Dani was on her way. Next stop—Yosemite Valley. It had been many years since she had visited the park with her church youth group, and the immensity of the towering granite cliffs and rushing Merced River renewed old memories. What a magnificent retreat the sheer walls offered to its visitors. She had read that two and a half million of them came every year, each making Yosemite his very own.

25

Dani purchased a Golden Eagle pass at the entrance station and congratulated herself that the young ranger didn't give her a second glance. Her disguise was a success. Hair pulled back into a severe bun. Horn-rimmed glasses. Drab gray blouse buttoned to the chin. Pleated skirt. Sensible lace-up shoes. No makeup. She was the picture of plainness. The ideal companion for a religious old woman. Talbott wouldn't even notice her as she went about gathering information.

She drove slowly down the valley road, gawking at the magnificent sights. El Capitan, Half Dome—silver walls of granite gouged out and polished by massive ice rivers thousands of years ago—wonderful!

Since it was still early, Dani stopped for a short visit in the village, noting the location of Park Headquarters, then made a brief stop at Yosemite Falls, her favorite place in the entire park.

The roar was deafening. An exceptionally heavy winter rainfall and spring melt in the High Sierra crashed over the black boulders sending white plumes spraying across the face of the mountain. Dani sat on a bench at the base of the falls and relished the cold spray on her cheeks. She pulled her jacket closer to her body, lifted her face, and closed her eyes. She learned something new—waterfalls don't just roar, they moan and clatter and rumble.

"You'll be drenched if you sit here long."

Dani's eyes flew open, startled to see she wasn't alone. A tall man dressed in faded blue jeans and denim jacket stood over her, smiling. His hair, the color of redwood bark, shone from the narrow rays of sun slanting through the trees, and his eyes, fringed with long mist-tipped lashes, twinkled with humor.

"It's a good way to wake up. I come here every morning."

She moved over on the bench as he sat down beside her. "Oh, do you live here?"

"Yes, this is my home. The 'Incomparable Valley.'" He spread his arms wide to take in the expanse. "Whoever named this place felt just as I do. It is incomparable!"

Dani lifted her eyes to the high cliffs and inhaled deeply. "I love it, too. It's been years since I've been here. I used to come with my church youth group. And before that, Mom and Dad came up every summer to camp. They have pictures of the 'old days' when burning embers were shoved off the edge of Glacier Point."

"Really?" The man laughed. "That must have been quite a sight."

Caught up in her memories, Dani went on, "Dad said that every night when it was dark, the people would stand out in the meadows and line up along the roadsides to hear the shout, 'Let the fire fall!' Then everyone cheered when the stream of red flowed over the point. It must have been exciting—"

She stopped midsentence when she realized the man was staring at her. His eyes flashed in the early morning sunlight, and she noticed little droplets of water clinging to his thick mustache. She must be getting wet, too. Glancing at her watch, she stood and excused herself.

"I think you have a beautiful home, but you were right . . ." She brushed at her jacket. "I am getting drenched." She reached into her pocket for the glasses and smoothed her hair. "I have to be going now. I have an appointment."

The man stood and bowed slightly. "Drop in again. This is a continuous show, and it's even wetter and more beautiful the closer you go." His smile showed even, white teeth, and Dani thought she hadn't met such an attractive, wholesome-looking man in a long time.

After asking directions at Park Headquarters, Dani

drove up a narrow service road marked with a sign, "Government Residential Area," and followed the road uphill until she came to a large two-story house. All of the buildings were painted the same tan color, but they were of various sizes and shapes, and the yards were landscaped according to the residents' preferences. Dani was pleased to see that the chief ranger's long front porch displayed tubs of bright red and yellow wildflowers. Someone there loved color.

"Miss Fuller?" A woman stood at the front door. Dani's first thought was that she was the housekeeper, but the woman quickly identified herself. "I'm Edna Talbott. Please come in."

Dani's surprise showed on her face. Edna Talbott was not the gray-haired old woman she expected, but a woman of about sixty with curly brown hair and large brown eyes. She was slim and dressed in gray slacks and a red blouse. Gold loop earrings shone through her curls, and Dani only sputtered as she tried to introduce herself. "I—ah—yes, I'm Miss Fuller. Dani. Well, my friends call me Dani, but my name is really Danielle. You can call me Dani."

Edna Talbott smiled with understanding and held out both hands. "Come in, dear. You've had a long trip and I'm sure you'd like to get on some dry things."

Self-consciously, Dani touched her damp hair and adjusted her glasses. She suddenly felt drab and old beside this youthful, vibrant woman.

"Would you like a cup of coffee first, or do you want me to show you to your room?"

"Forgive me for behaving so stupidly. I'm honestly surprised. I expected a much older, frail woman."

Edna patted Dani's arm. "I understand perfectly. My son portrays me as a poor, helpless old woman." She smiled again, obviously pleased with his concern for her. "It's true, though, I'm more helpless right now than I like to admit. I had a heart attack about a month ago, and need to take it easy for a while. Josh insisted I move in with him while I recuperate, and if that wasn't enough, he also insists I have a companion." She stopped to catch her breath and smiled again. "I admit I'm surprised, too. I expected an older woman as well. You're so young and attractive. Are you sure you want to spend your summer with the likes of me?"

For an instant, Dani forgot her purpose in coming and allowed her eyes to scan the beautifully decorated room with its floor to ceiling windows that brought the outdoors in. "I'm going to love being here." Her tone was sincere. "And I'm going to love being with you." Dani came to an instant conclusion. "I like you already, and want to help you all I can."

"Good, then the way you can help me right now is to get out of those wet clothes." She touched Dani's jacket with her fingertips. "For goodness sakes, it's not raining is it?"

"Oh, no, I just had to stop at Yosemite Falls before I came up." She rolled her eyes and smiled broadly. "Beautiful. Worth the wetness."

"That's what Josh says." Edna spoke over her shoulder as she led Dani toward a long hallway. "Come along now and I'll show you where you'll be sleeping. It's quite small," she apologized, "but feel free to have the run of the house."

She held up one finger. "With one exception. My son, Joshua, is a very private person. The upstairs is his domain. He hasn't hung a 'no trespassing' sign up there, but he may as well." She laughed and her eyes glowed with love. "Some people don't understand him—don't even like him, but I think you'll get along famously."

She patted Dani's arm. "You'll have to bring in your own bags, I'm afraid. Josh took off first thing this morning, and didn't say when he'd be back." Edna sighed and slumped her shoulders. "If you don't mind, I think I'll go lie down for a few minutes. Just make yourself at home."

Dani hung her clothes neatly in the closet, changed into dry clothes, redid her hair, and glanced at her watch. Since Edna was still sleeping soundly, Dani decided to take Edna's offer and check out the house.

It was almost noon and the sun streamed brightly through the windows, flooding the living room in a golden light. Dani walked slowly through the first floor, touching the highly polished table tops and pausing to admire the fine pieces of china and sculpture throughout the house. They must belong to Edna. Surely a man who made a career of tramping about the woods wouldn't have such exquisite taste.

She wondered again about the chief ranger. She already knew a little about him. If he was anything like his mother, he must be likeable. Yet if he was so private and demanding, he must have something to hide. He was probably a stick-in-the-mud bachelor, set in his ways. No wonder Edna was pleased to have a companion.

Dani glanced toward the stairs which led up to "never-never land." She passed by the tall windows, peering outside for any sign of life. The house, surrounded by ponderosa pines and oaks dotted with bulging green buds, stood apart from the other dwellings and sat back from the road. It was unusually quiet. Except for the occasional squawk of a bluejay, the silence seemed impenetrable.

She put one foot on the bottom stair and looked up. It was dark; the drapes must be drawn. Did she dare? She had to start spying sometime. She cocked her head again for outside noises and for any sound of movement from Edna's room, then before she could change her mind, she darted up the stairs, two at a time. With her heart pounding, she stopped on the landing to catch her breath.

Blinking to adjust to the darkness, she stepped cautiously into the large room that spread over the entire split-level upper floor. Her feet sank into thick carpeting as she crossed the room to where a walnut stereo cabinet dominated the corner. Plush cushions had been scattered on the floor, and stacks of tapes were arranged neatly on shelves.

By now Dani could see clearly. The room was absolutely elegant. What rich tastes. Costly belongings for a park ranger. Where did he get the money to buy such luxuries? Mark must be right—the chief ranger was an enigma. It was up to her to expose such lavish living, and discover how Joshua Talbott came to be so prosperous.

Dani tiptoed across the room to an oversized bed draped in a heavy velvet patchwork quilt. When she touched it, it swayed and swished. A waterbed! The man grew more interesting by the minute. Dani sat on the edge of the bed and felt the movement surround her. She had never been on one before. She scooted further back and flopped into the middle. What a sensation. It rolled and billowed under her like waves.

Putting her hands behind her head, she unfastened the clip in her hair, shook it free, and stretched out. Maybe she would get a waterbed someday. She closed her eyes and relaxed in the gentle movement, imagining herself as a wealthy San Francisco socialite. Perhaps after the sale of *Shadow on the Valley,* and a closer relationship with Mark Hutchinson, she might be able to afford such luxuries, too.

"What are you doing on my bed?"

Dani tried to sit up, her eyes wide with fear. Standing over her was the tall dark-haired man in faded blue jeans and denim jacket.

31

CHAPTER 3

"You!" they said in unison.

The man's brown eyes narrowed in anger, then he stepped closer. "Just what do you think you're doing on my bed?"

Dani fumbled to pull her hair back into the clip and smooth her skirt while she bounced and splashed her way to the edge. "This is *your* bed?" She teetered inelegantly as she continued to adjust her clothes. "Then you must be—Joshua Talbott!" Her words sputtered in a most undignified manner, and she stood as tall as she could and demanded, "Well, why didn't you say who you were—at the waterfall?"

The tall man folded his arms across his broad chest and glared. "It's your identity in question at the moment. Who are you, and what are you doing in my room?"

She lifted her chin, almost losing her balance. The man stood so close and towered so high over her that it hurt her neck to look up at him.

"If you'll be kind enough to step back, I'll explain my presence," she said with icy formality.

Joshua Talbott placed both hands on his hips and retreated only a few inches. "That would be refreshing. Explain."

"I'm Danielle Fuller, your mother's companion, and I do apologize for invading your privacy." She fingered the collar of her blouse. "Mrs. Talbott said I should look around the place while she took a nap."

"She didn't tell you the upstairs is off-limits?"

"If she did, I don't remember," Dani lied. "I'm sorry I startled you. It won't happen again." She could hardly stand her fawning tone, but she thought the ranger's eyes had softened, then his lips parted to reveal a mocking smile.

"Oh, I'm sure of that. I don't take well to trespassing."

She watched him slowly unbutton his jacket and toss it on the bed and thought again that although Joshua Talbott was hostile, he was definitely one of the most attractive men she had ever met.

About to start down the stairs, Dani was surprised to find him beside her. "Let's see if Mother is awake. I think Martha has our lunch ready."

Shoulders and chin held high, she marched beside him down the stairs, through the spacious living room, and down the long hallway to Edna Talbott's room. They didn't speak, but she had a feeling that his eyes were appraising her.

When they reached Edna's room, they found her sitting by the window in a rocking chair with a Bible on her lap. She looked up, a slight smile on her lips. "Oh, good. I see you two have met."

Dani wasn't too sure about the "good" part, but she fixed a smile on her face and kept her eyes on Joshua as he ambled across the room and held out his hands to his mother.

"Have a good nap?" he asked softly, brushing his lips over her forehead.

Edna nodded and flipped her head in a way that made her curls bounce, then linked her arm through his.

"Come along, dear." She smiled over her shoulder at Dani. "Let's get better acquainted. I know we're all going to be one happy family. Aren't we, Josh?" She smiled up at him as he helped her sit in the ladder-back chair at the kitchen table.

Dani sat down quickly and directed her words to Edna. "I hope I'll be able to fit in without causing too much trouble." She glanced in Joshua's direction. "It can be a little strange having someone new in your home."

"Not at all," Edna insisted. "Besides, you're not the only new one. I've been here less than a month— and so has Martha." She reached across the small round table and patted her son's hand. "Poor Joshua. It looks like his bachelor pad has been invaded."

"It's okay, you just get well." His voice was stern. "I'm glad you can be here where I can keep an eye on you, and as far as the 'help' is concerned—it's necessary."

He had put Dani in her place, and his eyes met hers for a minute as if to say, "Touché!"

Edna, unaware of the silent battle between them, spoke with a note of brightness, "Let's hold hands now and say grace." Before Dani could respond, Edna bowed her head and reached for Dani's hand. Reluctantly she surrendered the other into Joshua Talbott's long, strong fingers. His grip was steady and warm, and Dani felt a strange glow that began at her fingertips and crept up to her cheeks like two burning embers. What was wrong with her? Was it the remembrance of the love and warmth of her own Christian home, or was it—him?

When Edna finished praying, she stared at Dani with concern. "Now I do believe you're catching a cold. Your face is flushed and you're shaking." She glanced at her son who watched with interest. "Miss Fuller came in with wet hair and clothes this morning," she explained. "She's as bad as you—absolutely captivated by Yosemite Falls."

"Is that so?" Josh asked, lifting his chin. His eyes seemed to burn through Dani's, but she didn't back down.

"Yes, as a matter of fact, I had a pleasant conversation with a man there this morning. He made me feel quite at home here. Of course, you can never tell about a person at a first meeting. I really thought he was warm and friendly."

Josh's eyes were still on Dani. "You're right. It's hard to tell what a person is really like until you get to know them. I'm very careful about first impressions."

Dani glanced down at her plate, then at Edna. "I learn a lot from first impressions." She smiled at the older woman. "I knew right away that I liked you."

"And I like you, young lady. We both do. Josh . . ." Edna winked at him. "Dani is going to suit me wonderfully. I think you knew what you were doing when you hired a companion, after all."

"H'm, we'll see," he mumbled before rising from the table. "I'm afraid Miss Fuller might find it quite boring here. It probably isn't at all as she remembers it when she was a teenager."

"Oh, what . . . ?"

Josh didn't let his mother finish her question, instead he laid a typed schedule on the table in front of Dani.

"These are your duties." He pointed out each item. "See that Mother walks at least twenty minutes a day, takes plenty of naps, and sticks to this 'Prudent Diet.' "

He leaned over her with his arm resting on the back of the chair. How she wished he would leave the room so she could relax for a few minutes and get her emotions under control.

The jangling of the telephone ended Joshua's instructions, and he excused himself to race down the hall to the study. Edna shook her head. "He gets so many phone calls here at home and never mentions who called." She seemed to be talking to herself more than to Dani. "I do hope everything's all right. He's not himself lately."

Dani leaned forward in her chair. "Really? Do you think he might just be worried about you?" She hoped Edna would say more about her son. Mark would be pleased if on her first day in Yosemite, she discovered something revealing about the chief ranger.

Edna smiled sheepishly. "Oh, I'm sure he's concerned about me, but I really think it might be a woman." Pride shone in her eyes. "There's no reason for him to talk to me about his private life—after all, he's a grown man. Been on his own many, many years." A hint of a smile crinkled her large brown eyes. "No, I wouldn't be surprised if there was a woman—he *is* good looking, don't you think?"

Trying to sound indifferent, but again feeling her face grow hot, Dani mumbled, "Yes, I guess he is."

"Of course, this is his mother talking," Edna rambled on, "but I think he's handsome enough to be a movie star." She folded her hands in front of her and lowered her voice, "But don't tell him I said that. He already thinks I 'mother' him too much."

"He seems very devoted to you," Dani said, as she rinsed the plates and stacked them in the dishwasher. "He must have been terribly worried when you had a heart attack."

"Yes, he was. He's had more than his share of grief anyway, and you know, he had only recently moved here from Washington. Just getting used to the new responsibilities and all." She paused. "It has been hard on him."

37

Edna pushed back her chair and stood up. "Would you believe it's time for me to have another nap? I didn't sleep this much when I was a baby!" She laughed and slipped her arm through Dani's as they walked the short distance down the hall to her room, then before going in, she said, "Try not to take Josh too seriously, he can be quite a tease."

Dani didn't have to be told that. He obviously enjoyed her discomfort, first in the bedroom, then again at the table. They had gotten off to a bad start, and she would have to be more careful from now on. After all, she was here to investigate, not alienate him.

Dani looked around her small bedroom situated next to Edna's. It was bright and cheery with sun streaming through sheer curtains, painting designs of orange and yellow across the bedspread. There was a small desk where Dani had stacked her notebooks, her daily journal, and a copy of Mark's latest book and in the corner a chair with a matching ottoman. She would be comfortable here, and later this evening she would outline her plan for uncovering information and photographing the house. Those expensive items of china and furnishings would be of interest to Mark.

"Miss Fuller?" The chief ranger peered around the door. "I'd like to talk to you for a few minutes." He lowered his voice. "I see Mother's asleep, so I'd like to get a few things settled at the outset."

Without waiting for an invitation, he walked into the room and sat on the edge of the bed. "Since you're going to be living here for the next couple of months, and we didn't get off to a particularly good beginning, let's start over."

She nodded and sank to the ottoman, regarding him with caution.

"I'm glad you've come," he said. "I can see Mother likes you . . ." He paused, his eyes scrutinizing her. "And you seem to be just what the doctor ordered—a sensible, no-frills type. Unusual for a woman your age," he commented, still studying her.

"Besides," he said, a smile spreading across his face, "anyone who loves Yosemite Falls enough to get drenched early in the morning couldn't be all bad."

As Joshua Talbott laughed softly, Dani glanced past him to the small mirror that hung over the dresser. She did have a matronly look. No makeup, severe hairstyle, and tailored clothes. She pushed the glasses higher on her nose and smiled inwardly. Never in her life had she been called "a sensible, no-frills type." Of course, she did think of herself as sensible, but she loved all the frills of living in San Francisco.

"Thank you, Mr. Talbott," she said, ignoring his comment about their earlier meeting. "I hope I can be of help."

"I'm sure you can," he said, imitating her formal tone. "We got off to a bad start. Well, actually our start was fine, but Act Two wasn't great. I'm not accustomed to young women visiting my room." Josh stifled a yawn. "Excuse me, I've been up all night. One of our rangers was in an automobile accident, and I spent the night at the hospital in Mariposa."

Without warning, a veil of weariness came over him and he sighed. "I'm glad to have someone here now. I have to be away so much." He adjusted his tall frame in the center of the twin-sized bed and stretched out, his arms behind his head. She watched in amazement as he closed his eyes and seemed to settle down for a nap. Unconcerned that he was in her room, he opened his eyes a crack and smiled. "You may as well drop that 'Mr. Talbott' stuff as long as we're living in the same house. My friends call me Josh. Okay if I call you Dani?"

As he spoke her name, a fluttery feeling began

somewhere deep inside and she folded her arms in front of her. "That's my name, at least that's what my friends call me . . ." She paused. "I guess this means we're friends." A smile lit her face.

He leaned up on one elbow and returned her smile.

Dani allowed her eyes to sweep over him for a brief moment before speaking in a gruff voice, "By the way, who is this sleeping on *my* bed?"

With a start, Josh swung his feet to the floor and stretched his arms over his head. "Sorry about that. I've been burning the candle at both ends lately. Time to get going." He smiled as he reached the door. "Thanks for coming. I think you'll fit in just fine."

She attempted an answer, but a strange sensation washed over her. Perhaps she was coming down with a cold after all.

The days of the following week seemed to trip over each other as Dani settled into her new surroundings. She found herself strongly attracted to Edna and hated having to spy on her son. She hadn't wanted to get involved with these people; it would only make her deception that much harder. She was glad that Josh spent very little time at home. He was working extra shifts to fill in for that ranger who had been in the car crash.

"Most of his days," Edna explained, "are spent in the field—surveying trailheads and backroads for needed repairs."

To Dani, that seemed an unusual job for the chief ranger. She thought most of his time would be spent in the office. How she would like to get into his office. One day soon . . .

"I'd sure like to get out of the house for a while," Edna blurted out on Dani's first Saturday morning. "I had a good night's sleep, and as much as I love this beautiful house, a change in scenery is in order."

40

Dani smiled at the woman's reflection in the mirror. She had just washed Edna's hair and waved the blow dryer over the soft curls. Edna's face did look more relaxed and her eyes brighter as she brushed a soft glow of pink blush over her cheeks.

"Oh, I think you should get out of the house, and let the tourists see what a beautiful mother the chief ranger has." Dani rested her hands on Edna's shoulders after buttoning up the back of her blouse. "You look great today!"

"And so do you," Edna said, standing up to face Dani. "You've only been here a week, and already I can see that the mountain air is doing you good." She cocked her head and smiled. "I just wish that son of mine would spend more time at home. I think the two of you have a lot in common."

"Come on, Edna, you're not playing Cupid, are you?" Dani turned to leave the room.

"You are unattached, aren't you?"

"Well, yes, but . . ."

"All right, just hear me out. I see you gazing out the window at the pines like you were in a cathedral. You love this place already. I've watched you browse through the books in the library and noticed that you read right through that volume of poetry Josh has been looking at."

"You've been spying on me." Dani shook her forefinger at Edna and smiled. "Are you trying to say I'm your son's type? Come on, Edna, take another look."

"I'm not saying anything yet, but if you read the same books and view the wilderness with the same expression of awe . . ."

"Aw," Dani teased, "let's take that walk."

They decided to play tourist and walk the short distance to the Visitor Center in Yosemite Village. Perhaps Dani could learn more about the chief ranger

41

if she wandered around awhile listening to other rangers and watching them in action.

While Edna was in rapt attention watching a presentation on the geologic extravaganza that had formed Yosemite Valley, Dani mingled among those near the book racks. She chose a book that was filled with maps and information on trails, imagining the joy of hiking the high country. Maybe one day she and Mark would hike these trails.

"And how is Goody-Two-Shoes today?"

Dani whirled, her eyes fiery. "What are you doing here?"

"Looking for you." Ken Bridges' pale blue eyes raked over her. "I wouldn't have recognized our 'enterprising' young sleuth if it hadn't been for those curves you can't seem to hide."

Dani glanced toward Edna Talbott. "You'd better get out of here, or you'll blow my cover for sure." She was even beginning to sound like a spy.

"Hutchinson wants you to call—today," he growled. "That is if you're doing your job."

Dani buried her face in a book, still shaking with anger. When she looked up, the man had disappeared as quickly and quietly as a cockroach.

It was an hour later when Dani placed her call to San Francisco. She had made an excuse to go back to the village for milk, then found the public phone near the post office. Her thoughts of Edna Talbott and Ken Bridges dissolved in her excitement to hear Mark's voice. Finally, he came on the line. "Dani, I'm so glad you called. Is everything going well up there?"

She could imagine the tall, slim man, a view of the San Francisco skyline behind him, sitting at his desk lighting a cigarette. A wave passed over her. She dismissed it as homesickness, but enjoyed picturing the deep gray eyes of her employer. "I think so, Mark. I haven't found out anything unusual yet—

except our chief ranger seems to have possessions he couldn't possibly afford on his salary."

"Oh?"

"His home is lavish," she went on, "collector's items, rare pieces of china, Oriental rugs and he's gone most of the time."

"Any chance to look into his private papers?"

"Not yet. I'll have to be extremely careful. He caught me in his room my first day here."

Mark whistled. "Better watch yourself. Find anything?"

"Only a waterbed."

Mark's tone was cool. "Don't lose your objectivity. Get involved—but not too involved!"

Dani felt a warmth of embarrassment at his inference. "Don't worry," she sighed. "My presence here is strictly business—all the way around!"

"Good." His mood changed. "By the way, I'm going to drive to Fresno tomorrow, and after I've finished my business there, I'll have a couple of free days. Do you suppose you could get away a day or two? We could meet at the Yosemite Wawona Hotel."

Mark explained that the hotel was on Wawona Road, about twenty-five miles south of Yosemite Valley. She wouldn't be recognized there, and they could go over any information she had gathered. "Don't forget, you're there for one reason—to burn Talbott and the Park Service."

It all sounded so ugly. She wished she had never agreed to come, but tried to sound professional. "I'll see what I can do and call you back."

"Great, and Dani . . ." His tone was soft and seductive. "I'm looking forward to seeing you again. You were a feast for the eyes in this office!"

As she replaced the receiver, she thought, *Were, is right. It'll be a treat to shed these drab clothes and dress up again!*

When Dani arrived back at the Talbott's home, she found Edna still crocheting her blue afghan. Dropping down on the floor in front of her, Dani's eyes glowed with excitement.

"Well," Edna said, smiling brightly, "I've never seen anyone so happy over a carton of milk."

Dani laughed at the realization that she had come back empty-handed.

"That *is* why you left, isn't it?"

She looked up into the older woman's face and confessed, "I'm afraid I wasn't totally honest with you, Edna. I didn't go back to the village for milk; I have a special friend who wanted me to call him."

"So there is an attachment after all. I knew there must be a man in your life. All right, tell me about your friend."

Dani's mind raced ahead to think of a plausible story. "He lives in San Francisco and has to be in Fresno on business for a few days. He'd like me to meet him there—if it can be arranged." Dani hurried on. "We'll be staying with his aunt," she lied. "I wouldn't want you to think badly of me."

Edna smiled down at her and laid aside her handwork. "How could I? From what I've seen in a very short time, you are a lovely Christian girl who's strayed a little, but," she said, patting Dani's hand, "you'll find your way back." A tear glistened in the corner of her eye. "You're so like Josh. He's a Christian too, you know—been hurt badly, but it will heal. God is good."

Dani's eyes widened at the news of his relationship with God, but she wasn't too surprised. She had sensed a strength in his life and manner that reminded her of her dad. She slipped off her glasses, and at the same time, her hair fell out of its clip and cascaded over her shoulders around her small oval face. With clear blue eyes still fastened on Edna, she asked, "What hurt him?"

44

Edna's eyes seemed to be looking into the past as she lowered her voice and said, "Joshua wouldn't want me to talk about it, but I'll tell you this much—there was a terrible accident, and . . ." She pressed her lips together as if to blot out the memory.

Dani ached for the sadness she saw in Edna's face, and took both hands in hers and held them to her lips. "I'm sorry I pried into something painful for you. Will you forgive me?"

Edna's eyes brightened as she looked up to see Josh stroll into the room. He plopped onto the couch next to his mother.

"What's going on here?" he asked, focusing his attention on Dani seated at his feet. "Is this a hen session, or can I get in on it?"

His leg, hard and sinewy, rested against Dani's arm. There it was—that thrill again. She knew by now that she didn't have a cold. She had a crush on Joshua Talbott. She had tried to avoid him whenever possible. It was ridiculous, this giddy schoolgirl behavior, yet she couldn't help it. She blushed and trembled every time he came near.

She came back from her dreaming to hear Edna explain that Dani wanted a couple of days off to visit a boyfriend in Fresno. What must he think of her? Did he believe she was a "good" Christian girl, too?

"Sure." His tone chilled her. "Why not? We can get Martha to come in full-time while you're gone."

She looked up into the piercing brown eyes which seemed to penetrate her soul, to probe into the secret recesses where she had hidden. She made a movement to stand, and Josh held out his hands to help, then continued to hold her hands in his.

"What's different about you today?" He touched a curl that draped over her shoulder. "You let your hair down. I like it."

His gentleness moved her. His nearness. His touch.

Dani's heart pounded out of control. Then without warning, his expression changed and he turned to leave the room. "Don't worry about a thing. I'll get Martha—you go meet your friend. But," he added, "remember, you have a responsibility here. After this, have him come to you."

Later that night after Edna had gone to sleep, Dani stepped out on the porch to take one last look at the full moon. The giant ponderosa pines swayed gently in the breezes, creating feathery silhouettes against the moonlit sky. Where had Josh gone so soon after their conversation? Was he meeting a woman, or was he involved in some kind of business deal as Mark suspected? She remembered overhearing him discuss large sums of money with one of his rangers, Bill McCall. They were talking about a million dollars needed for repairs. Could they be planning to use the money for something else? Her thoughts rolled around in her head, bouncing off ideas like a pinball machine. She shook her head. Now she was even making things up in her mind. Joshua Talbott was so clean, he squeaked!

Feeling the need to get away from the house for a few minutes, she tiptoed to Edna's room and listened to her soft breathing, then changed from her gown and robe into jeans and sweatshirt. Just a few minutes at Mirror Lake would help her to think straight. It was usually quiet there, a kind of retreat through the looking glass.

When Dani reached the parking area, which was closed to visitors, it was vacant except for a couple of cars parked in the shadows of overhanging trees. She filled her lungs with the cool night air, reveling in the rich piney fragrance mixed with damp mosses that grew luxuriantly underfoot, then made her way down the narrow path that led to the water's edge. A light wind scarcely ruffled the glassy surface which reflected not only the full moon but the imposing might of Mount Watkins.

Wonderful. Just what she needed. Somehow sharing the night with only the trees and God's creation filled her with hope—hope that there was more to life than trying to get ahead. She surprised herself with thoughts of God. She had been thinking of him more since coming to Yosemite than in all the years since leaving home. He was real, and she was beginning to think he really cared for her, even though she had strayed from his paths. Edna's life was an example to her, and after hearing of Josh's faith, she could see that they might have more in common than she imagined.

Not wanting to be away from Edna for long, Dani turned away from the peaceful scene to leave. Sounds of muffled voices drifted to her ears from around a slight bend. A young couple must be enjoying a romantic rendevous. She smiled to herself as she thought what a lovely place it was to fall in love. Her smile quickly froze as a familiar voice reached her ears. Joshua Talbott! What was he doing at Mirror Lake? She knew he wasn't on duty tonight. Perhaps she had stumbled onto his secret.

Her conscience told her to put one foot in front of the other and forget her suspicions—but her duty to her job held her in her tracks. She stooped down behind a shrub and tipped her head to one side, listening for another voice. A woman. A woman whose voice she had heard many times before. It was Betty McCall, Bill's wife. Dani didn't know her well, but she had spoken with her when she had come on her daily visits to see Edna. At least that was her excuse for coming.

Was she involved with the chief ranger? The thought was preposterous. Unthinkable. Yet what did she really know about Joshua's private life? Only what she had learned from his mother, and what mother knows all her son's secrets?

Edna! Dani had better get back to the house before Joshua discovered her here. Suddenly, she felt guilty for betraying Edna's trust, and Joshua's too.

CHAPTER 4

"IS THAT YOU, JOSHUA?" Edna called from her room.

"No, it's just me." Dani poked her head around the door. "I went out for a breath of fresh air, but now I'm going to bed." She walked over to Edna. "You okay?"

"Yes, I just woke up and wondered if Josh had come in yet. Do you know if he has?"

"I imagine he's sound asleep by now. You just stop worrying and get a good night's rest." Poor Edna. She probably suspected Josh's philandering, but did she have any idea who he was involved with?

After crawling into bed, Dani tossed and turned trying to find sleep, but instead men and women from the past paraded across her subconscious. Sunday school teachers, ministers, missionaries, even Edna and Josh. They all pointed at her and chanted the same questions. "Where are you going, Dani? Who are you, anyway? A spy! A spy!"

Much later, she wasn't sure how long, Dani sat up and rubbed her eyes, wondering if Josh had come in.

With Bill off in San Francisco at the regional offices, Josh had evidently taken the opportunity to be alone with Betty. Dani felt disappointed. Betty just didn't seem the type, so wholesome and sweet.

Instead of struggling to fall asleep, she decided to go to the kitchen for a glass of milk. On her way, she noticed that the front porch light still shone brightly. Josh hadn't returned home yet, and it was after midnight. She padded her way down the hall and through the living room, the soft carpet caressing her bare feet. She stopped at the foot of the stairs and looked up. Should she give it another try? After all, she was here to research Joshua Talbott; what better place than his own room?

Her chin jutted out in determination and her lips pressed tightly together as she hiked up the skirt of her nightgown and flew up the stairs—a streak of shimmery blue lightning.

Straining to remember how the furniture was arranged, she carefully felt her way around the room. It would be like her to knock something over and wake Edna, or stub a toe. She always screamed when she stubbed her toe. She must be careful.

How strange the room felt. Even though Josh wasn't present, she could sense him. Spicy aftershave. Leather belts and shoes, man scents, fresh and outdoorsy. Dani swung open the closet doors, which covered an entire wall, and flicked on a nearby switch, lighting up the immense walk-in closet. She gasped in surprise.

Women's clothes!

At least half the closet was filled with women's clothes. Beautiful clothes. Silks, imported woolens, cashmere, even fur coats packaged in airtight wrappings. What could it mean?

She lifted a hanger from the rod and examined a tweed suit. Its narrow cut could fit a slim woman, but the length of the arms and skirt were obviously for someone much taller than Edna Talbott. Whose were they?

Thoughtfully, she replaced the hanger on the rod, then stood on her tiptoes and reached for a hatbox on the shelf. Her long silky gown brushed against her ankles as a thin spaghetti strap slipped off her shoulder. Before she had a chance to adjust it —she was swept off her feet and dumped into the middle of the bed!

Swaying with the movement of the water, she leaned up on one elbow and peered through a long strand of hair into the face of Joshua Talbott. He didn't speak, but she could feel his dark brown eyes burn through her like live coals. His breath came in long uneven sighs, and she wished he'd say something—anything. Then maybe she could think up an answer.

Then tension eased, and his first words were gentle, almost seductive. "I don't know why you keep visiting my room . . ." He waited as if trying to decide what to say next. "I don't know what you're up to. I don't even know who you are. It's obvious you're not the little Plain Jane you've pretended to be."

He stepped around to the foot of the bed where Dani struggled to stand up and held out a large hand. She refused it, finally reaching the edge. She stood up, folding her arms in front of her.

"I know how this must look," she said, backing away. "But I came up here to see . . . to see if I could find an extra blanket. I was chilled tonight." Dani hoped she sounded convincing. "There weren't any in the downstairs closet."

Josh nodded. "I'm not surprised you were cold— dressed like that." He tipped his head toward the bed. "You can share my blanket."

51

"I don't want your blanket. Though I know this looks awkward, I really don't want anything to do with you."

"Oh? I guess you're only interested in your boyfriend, and your rendezvous in Fresno." His tone was mocking and his eyes raked over her.

"Josh—Mr. Talbott," she stuttered. "My personal life could be of no possible interest to you, and as far as you're concerned, you hired me as a companion to your mother, and I'm doing my best to help her in her recovery." She sighed. "But since you seem to have very little respect for me, I'll understand if you want me to leave."

As Josh stepped closer, she found it very difficult to project sternness. If she moved backward, she would fall across the bed. If she moved an inch closer, her nose would be against his chest. "Let me pass, please."

Josh held his ground. With the back of his hand, he gently brushed her flushed cheeks. His touch, even the softness in his eyes, was a complete reversal. "I just want to know who you are. You've made me wonder if I've met the real Danielle Fuller."

Dani was overwhelmed. She couldn't speak, couldn't move. As he continued to look into her eyes, she tilted her head and closed her eyes, waiting. But instead of a kiss, Josh stepped back and nudged her toward the stairs. "You better get out of here—and don't come back."

"You mean—I'm fired?"

White teeth flashed under the dark mustache for an instant before he spoke in a gruff voice. "No, I want you to stay. Mother's come to depend on you. But, if you ever come into this room *uninvited* again, you will be fired."

The next day passed without the slightest glimpse of Josh. Dani felt numb as she went about her duties, and was only able to get through them by anticipating her meeting with Mark. At least with him, she'd be on familiar ground. So far, she had botched her assignment and wouldn't be surprised if *he* threatened to fire her, too.

Later that evening, after Dani had packed a few things for her two-day trip and had prepared for bed, Edna called her into her room.

"I've been talking with the Lord," she said with a sweet smile and wide brown eyes, "and I think he wants me to have a little talk with you, too." She sat on the edge of her bed and patted the place next to her. "I can see there's something bothering you, and I hope you can trust me enough to talk about it. I'm a good listener, and never tell anyone what I hear, except the Lord, of course."

Dani felt the tears well up behind her eyelids. She wanted to talk to someone, but she couldn't tell Edna that she had come under false pretenses—to spy on her son. She couldn't tell anyone.

Edna went on, her tone sober. "God knows all about you, dear, and he has a wonderful life planned. You don't want to miss out on his best, do you?"

A tear trickled down Dani's face, and she cleared her throat. Still when she spoke her voice was husky. "I know God loves me, Edna, and I love him. It's just that I, well, I thought I could run my own life."

She groaned. "Seems I've made a mess of it though. Now it's too late—I've just got to straighten things out for myself."

A sob escaped her lips, and Edna opened her arms. As the older woman embraced her, a sense of peace eased the pain.

Edna spoke softly, "Dear Lord, I ask you to show this child what path to take. Give her courage to do your will."

Dani gave Edna a squeeze and started to leave the room when Edna added, "I'm praying the same prayer for my son. You're more alike than either of you knows."

Early the next morning, Dani dressed in tailored slacks and a high-collared blouse, a "sensible, no-frills" outfit, tossed a few last minute things into her suitcase and glanced at the small clock beside her bed. It was eight o'clock, and Mark wasn't expecting her at Wawona until around four. There was time to do a little long-awaited sightseeing. She kissed Edna good-by, glad that Josh was nowhere in sight, and pulled away from the large house that had become her home. First stop—Yosemite Falls.

As spring became summer, the population in the valley grew. Bright blue rental bikes wove along the shoulder of the road and young people in jeans and hiking boots strode toward the trails, their backpacks bulging with supplies for their trips. Dani felt over-dressed in her tailored clothes, but reminded herself that she was on her way to a business engagement with a sophisticated publisher.

She joined the tourists as they gaped upward at the magnificent display of waterworks. The falls dropped almost 2,500 feet in three giant steps and put on an early summer display that was unequaled in beauty. Dani's mouth gaped open along with everyone's. She noticed people of many races and heard unfamiliar tongues spoken. People came from all over the world to see Yosemite Valley—and she had the privilege to live here.

After determining to climb the Yosemite Falls trail one day, she drove through the valley enjoying the change of seasons. Summer had come on gradually. Wildflowers had begun to fade, the airy blooms of dogwood were no longer visible, and the fragrant azalea that had been blooming along the streams had completed its show. Dani felt a new season was beginning in her life, too. She liked herself.

She turned up the road that led to Glacier Point. Her trip to the point took hours longer than she had planned because she stopped every few minutes to take pictures, although not exactly the kind Mark expected. She loved the sight from Discovery View. The trees obscured all the roads and buildings, and Dani thought the valley must look as it did to the first white men who came to Yosemite. Only a little crease in the planet, a few miles long and one mile wide, its beauty had hypnotized thousands year after year. It was not only Joshua Talbott's "Incomparable Valley," it belonged to everyone.

Dani spent the rest of the day reveling in the awesomeness of canyons and waterfalls, meadows and mule deer. She began to wonder if she could return to San Francisco after touching such handiwork. As she followed the curving road, she pondered how it would be to see Mark. Although only a couple of weeks had passed, so much had happened.

After many winding miles, the road opened up into the Wawona Valley. It reminded her of a country scene—a verdant meadow bathed in golden afternoon sunshine. A golf course spread out across the road from the hotel, bringing Dani back to the realization that she was no longer a sightseer. However, the hotel with its long, wide verandas that stretched the length of both upper and lower floors gave her the feeling that she had stepped back in time. Wawona Valley was different from Yosemite Valley. Not the hurry and bustle she'd found there, but a quiet and peaceful retreat.

As she drove into the parking lot, she spotted Mark's black Mercedes and pulled in next to it. She loosened her hair, dropped her glasses into her purse, and unfastened the top button of her blouse. Mark would be expecting his "enterprising" researcher, not a Plain-Jane companion of elderly women.

"Dani, I've been watching for you," Mark called from the porch. "You're a sight for sore eyes." He walked briskly across the length of the veranda and met her as she started up the steps. He took her suitcase and led her to the registration desk.

Dani was pleasantly surprised. Although the building was old, probably late 1800s vintage, the inside was quite modern.

She glanced at Mark as he spoke to the cashier. Even here he was as suave and hatbox perfect as in his plush San Francisco office, although he seemed more tense than she'd remembered. His eyes were harder and his lips thinner. He wasn't as handsome as she had painted him in her memory, either. Maybe her time with comfortable, uncomplicated people had opened her eyes to what city living does to the personality.

After a shower and short rest, Dani met Mark in the hotel dining room.

"The mountain air seems to have done you good," he said, slanting his eyes at her. "I don't think I've ever seen you look more vibrant."

"I don't think you've ever taken much of a look at me, Mr. Hutchinson. I'm only one of your many employees."

"Don't kid yourself, Miss Fuller. I've been looking you over for quite some time."

Dani felt the color rise to her cheeks. "You may be right about the climate. I love it up here!"

"Is that all?" Mark asked. "Or do I sense that our famous chief ranger has been charming you?"

Dani glanced over the menu, then set it down and rested her chin on her hands, prayer-fashion. "He's not the easiest person to get along with. I do think he's hiding something, which brings me to a question I've been wanting to ask. Why the interest in someone like a park ranger? Who cares what he does with his personal life? I can understand the public's interest in a governor or movie star—but a ranger in a national park?"

Mark gave the waitress their order, then leaned back and lit a cigarette. "That's just the point. Everyone exposes the big wheel. My books show that the so-called little guy is just as corruptible—especially in government positions." Mark stared at her. "I *hope* you've read my books, and are convinced that wherever you look, you can find people out for the almighty buck."

"Even in the publishing business?" Dani smiled, and the dimple in her cheek caught Mark's eye.

"Sure," he said, inhaling deeply and allowing his eyes to rest upon her lips. "I admit I'm interested in money, too, but I won't cheat the taxpayer to get it."

They paused in their conversation as the waitress set their dinners before them.

"Oh, by the way . . ." Mark's voice broke with a chuckle. "I hear you and Bridges had a cozy dinner in Mariposa's favorite 'greasy spoon.'"

Dani shuddered as she recalled that meeting. "Let's get back to my question—why Talbott? As far as I can tell, even if he's involved with another man's wife, and has a closet full of women's clothes, who cares?"

She had dropped her scoop right in his lap and smiled as she waited for him to pick it up.

Mark's eyes flew open and he almost dropped his steak knife. "He *what?* A homewrecker and who knows what else? Fantastic! Danielle Fuller, I could kiss you!"

Dani's face flushed, whether with embarrassment or pleasure, she didn't know. "Well, I can't be sure of his involvement yet. I need to check further, and the clothes—h'm, if you print any of this before I'm certain, I'll sue!"

"Hey, hey, not so quick to fight! You sound like you're on his side." He shook his head. "That's the wrong side, baby."

She stabbed a flowerlet of broccoli, shoving it to the side of her plate. "I'm not on anyone's side. I just want the truth. If Josh is doing something illegal, of course it should be exposed, but . . ." She paused and shrugged her shoulders. "I don't want to hurt innocent people."

"Say, you're not falling for the guy, are you?"

"Of course not," she answered too quickly. "It's his mother I'm thinking of. Edna is a jewel. I wouldn't want to hurt her. Her son is her life."

"Well, don't worry. If he's innocent—of graft, I mean—even if he's fooling around, we won't expose it unless we think he's misrepresenting the National Park Service. Don't forget—ninety-three percent of all consumer legislation was originally stimulated by written exposés. We're doing the citizens a favor!" Mark rubbed his smooth chin. "A closet full of women's clothes, huh? What do you suppose that means?"

"I don't know, but he caught me looking at them and was awfully angry." She felt her heart flutter as she recalled the intimate scene.

When they finished their dinner, they sauntered out to the veranda to relax on chaise lounges. Lost in their own thoughts, they didn't speak for several minutes, then Mark leaned forward and said, "That guy is up to something, and I want to know what."

"Do you have any other leads? Surely you've done some investigation into his past."

"As a matter of fact, Bridges has come up with a

few discoveries on his own. He's traced down a wife—and rumors about an accident.''

The blood drained from Dani's face. "He's married?''

''Maybe divorced. Maybe widowed. I really don't know. Couldn't you pump the old lady? Might give us some answers about those clothes.''

Dani flinched at the disrespect. ''No, Edna won't talk about Josh's past. She did mention that he's been hurt, but that's all she'll say. They have a lot of family loyalty.''

She was proud to say it. Her family would stick by her, too. They wouldn't divulge her past to curious bystanders, either.

Mark interrupted her thoughts. ''Ken has sources that suggest Talbott may be paying through the nose. Lots of cash leaving his bank account. Blackmail, maybe.''

Dani bit the edge of her lower lip. Her blue eyes were round and moist. ''That's hard to believe, but I'll look into it. I have to admit, Mark, I'm curious about his expensive furnishings.''

After several quiet minutes, Mark stretched his arms over his head and stood up, a tall angular shadow on the darkened veranda. He peered closely at his watch, then at her. ''How about a nightcap in my room? I've rented a suite, and it's quite comfortable.'' He slapped the back of his neck. ''Besides, the mosquitos have gathered for the attack.''

Alone in his room? No way. Dani wasn't about to get herself into another predicament. ''Thanks, Mark, but I'm really tired. I think a good night's sleep will do me more good.''

She led the way back into the lighted foyer and started up the stairs. When they reached her room, she turned to face him, one hand on the doorknob. ''I enjoyed the dinner and appreciate your patience with my investigation. I have an idea how to track down his expenditures, and maybe I can come up with the exposé you're looking for." She didn't feel as enthusiastic as she sounded, but he seemed satisfied.

"You sure you don't want me to come in?" He leaned over and covered her hand with his. "We could talk a little longer about this project, and who knows what else might develop?" The expression on his face left no doubt about his intentions.

"I think you have the wrong idea about me," she said, inserting the key in the lock. "I'm strictly an employee, a lowly research assistant—"

"You could be more with just a little effort."

"Mr. Hutchinson!" Her voice was crisp. "Let's not complicate our relationship. I'm happy with my job and like working for you, but—"

"You think of me only as a boss." He frowned down at her.

"I like you as a person, too, but—"

He interrupted her again. "And I like you."

With those words, and in one smooth movement, Mark Hutchinson slipped into the room, shut the door behind them, and gathered Dani into his arms. Before she could resist, his lips were on hers, hard and demanding. He held her close with a strength that frightened her.

With all her power, she pushed him away, then slapped his face. Her eyes flashed. "You have the wrong idea about me, Mr. Hutchinson. I'm not interested in extracurricular activities or nightcaps or anything else." Tears of anger welled up in her eyes. "Besides, I'm . . . a Christian!"

She'd said it. For too many years, she'd been a closet Christian, not wanting to wear a label. But suddenly she was glad to say why she was different. Why she had high ideals. Why she believed in the sanctity of marriage.

Mark stepped back and stared at her. The turndown was evidently a new experience for him. As he opened the door to leave, Dani repeated the words, "Yes, I'm a Christian, and if that's fanatic or unacceptable to you and Westcoast Publishing Company, then you'll just have to find yourself another woman for this assignment."

"Hold on there. I've no intention of burning you at the stake or feeding you to the lions." He rubbed the red spot on his cheek. "You can't blame a guy for trying. You are a lovely woman—and that dress doesn't hide it."

Dani felt ashamed. She had never before struck another human being. She touched his smooth cheek with her fingertips. "I'm sorry I hit you. You just got my Irish up."

Mark leaned toward her with a devilish glint in his eyes. "How about a kiss to make it well?"

"Get out of here," she said, a tight smile on her lips. "I'll see you in the morning."

But as she shut the door and leaned against it, a new plan formed in her mind.

CHAPTER 5

On a sheet of paper embossed with the words, "Wawona Hotel, Yosemite National Park," Dani scrawled, "Mark, I've an exciting idea for learning more about Talbott, and to accomplish it, I have to leave for the valley tonight. Sorry I can't spend more time with you but will contact you at your office some time next week."

With her suitcase in one hand and the letter in the other, she stopped briefly to speak to the night clerk, handed him the envelope, and walked briskly across the hardwood floor. The click of her high heels reminded her that she was still dressed for dinner, and the drive back to the valley would have been more comfortable in slacks and blouse. Never mind. The important thing was to arrive at home while Edna and Joshua still slept.

Driving through the darkness, Dani could visualize the office keys hanging in the kitchen cabinet behind the sugar canister. "Mother," Joshua had said one morning, "I'm leaving the keys to Park Headquarters here on this shelf." He had jangled them in the air before slipping them over an unused cup hook. "Just in case you need to get into my papers and I'm not available."

Edna had nodded absentmindedly, and Dani had been absorbed in a magazine article on coronary care. Not until this evening when Mark slipped into her room with such ease, did she remember the keys and the possibility of getting into Joshua's office. She could look over his personal correspondence. If Ken Bridges said large amounts of money were leaving Joshua's account, there must be proof in his bank statements.

Mile after mile, she plotted ways to sneak into the building to gather information implicating Joshua Talbott. If he was mismanaging government funds, he should be exposed, she reminded herself. On she sped through the Wawona Tunnel, past Discovery View, and down the road leading to the valley.

That's when she first noticed a car following closely behind her—so close and so fast that she pulled to the shoulder to give it passing room. The driver made no attempt to swerve around her, but stayed about ten feet back. Suddenly it sped up—and rammed her back bumper!

What was the idiot doing?

Another jarring thump. This time harder.

Someone was either trying to force her off the road or crush her back fender.

Dani's foot pressed heavily on the accelerator. Forty. Forty-five. She gripped the wheel with sweaty palms. Fifty miles an hour around the curves.

Still the car followed. After each jolt, it would drop back, almost out of sight, then speed up again. Bump!

Dani's heart hammered in her chest. Her neck, rigid with fear, ached with a dull pain. She licked her lips with a dry tongue and strained to see beyond the headlights of her car. The clock on her dashboard read 2:00. Was anyone else out this time of night? Campers, hikers, everyone in their right minds were snuggled down in sleeping bags by now.

Finally off Wawona Road and on the South Road leading past the turnoff to Bridalveil Falls, Dani spotted a green Yosemite Park truck.

She whipped off the road and hit her brakes. Gravel and dust spewed into the air, clattering against her windshield. She leaped out of the driver's seat and ran around to the side of the truck where a ranger was watching a deer. From the corner of her eye, Dani saw the pursuing car race by with its lights off—a dark indiscernible instrument of terror.

"Dani!" a voice exclaimed. "What's wrong? What are you doing here?"

"Oh, Josh, help me!"

She ran to his open arms and buried her face against the roughness of his green uniform. He held her long moments until the trembling subsided and her breath came in a slow, easy rhythm. They were enveloped in quietness with only the gentle moaning of breezes blowing through the branches of the evergreens and the muted roar of the Merced River as it thundered downstream. Gravel crunched as Josh shifted his position, and through his layers of clothes, Dani felt the pounding of his heart in unison with hers. Finally she looked up into his face, washed white with moonlight. His eyes were wide, his lips parted.

"Dani, tell me what's the matter?"

"Can we sit down? My knees are weak!"

With his arm still around her shoulders, he opened the door on the passenger side of the truck, and she climbed in and rested her head against the back of the seat. "I've never been so scared in my life," she groaned as he slid in beside her. "That car was chasing me down the mountain. I'll bet he dented my fender."

She moved as if to go check.

"Don't bother with that now." The crease in Josh's forehead deepened. "What car are you talking about? Why should someone be chasing you?" He shook his head in confusion. "And why are you out in the middle of the night?"

Silence.

What could she say? That she was on her way to Park Headquarters to go through his files? And how about that car? She'd been so terrified, she was sure she couldn't identify it.

Josh spoke again. "I thought you were going into Fresno today. What happened? What are you doing here?"

"Well," she stammered, "my friend sent word he couldn't make it after all." She shrugged her shoulders. "Our plans just didn't work out."

"Then why did you leave? Where have you been all day?"

Dani combed her mind for a plausible answer. "Since you'd given me the days off, and Martha had already come, I decided to do some sightseeing. I've fallen in love with your 'Incomparable Valley' and all I've seen of this magnificent park." She glanced up at Josh who still wore a frown, and continued, "Anyway, I went to Glacier Point, then drove to the Wawona Hotel for dinner. I planned to spend the night there but decided I'd sleep better in my own bed." She shook her head. "Crazy, huh?"

"A little." He smiled down at her. "But I still want to know why someone was chasing you."

"It was probably just some kid out for a thrill." Dani breathed deeply. "Anyway it's over now, and I thank you for saving me—my knight in green armor."

Dani caught her breath as Josh reached toward her and gently cupped her chin in his hand. This time she wouldn't close her eyes; instead she turned her head and climbed down from the truck, her knees weak from the emotion he stirred in her. "If you're ready to go home now, I'd sure appreciate a bodyguard!"

Josh turned the ignition on and nodded. "Sure thing. I'm just glad I was on duty tonight. If Phil hadn't sprained his ankle today, I'd have been in bed long ago."

Through her rearview mirror, Dani watched Joshua as he followed close behind. She had almost gotten herself into another unexplainable trap. Suppose she had taken the keys and gone to his office thinking he was home asleep. Suppose he had dropped by headquarters when he went off duty. Suppose he caught her once more in a place she didn't belong.

They parked in front of the house and walked side by side up the narrow walk. Josh unlocked the door and switched on the lamp by the sofa.

An unruly brown curl drooped over his high forehead entangling itself in long dark lashes. Dani had a strong urge to touch it, to twist it around her finger, then allow her hands to hold his head against her chest.

"How about a cup of coffee?" His smile emphasized the creases in his cheeks. "I sure could go for one. You gave me quite a scare—did you see that deer make for cover?"

Dani felt an instant replay of fear that washed away her fantasies. Who would do such a thing? Mark? Was he angry that she had left? No, he'd never abuse his Mercedes that way. But who? And why?

"Dani? How about it—coffee?"

"I'd rather have a glass of milk. I've had enough excitement to keep me awake for the rest of the night." She rubbed her hands together. "In fact, I'm hungry again. Would you like something to eat?"

Without another word, she stepped out of her shoes, padded into the kitchen, and reached behind the door for an apron to tie around her waist. Josh followed closely behind, watching her every move. His eyes were soft and warm as he appraised her from across the room. "That's a nice dress. Silk, isn't it?"

"Yes. My one and only." She curtsied. It was the first time Josh had seen Dani wear something other than her "sensible" clothes.

"You look good in that color. Matches your eyes." His expression was one of obvious, unveiled admiration.

Her face warmed under his gaze and she thought she'd never heard a more sincere compliment on her turquoise dress.

"Thanks," she said, glancing down to see if the V-neck plunged too deeply. "I only wear it on special occasions."

"Then let's make this a special one." Josh reached for the china plates stored on the top shelf and grabbed two crystal goblets. "For scrambled eggs and milk."

His smile erased their previous misunderstandings, and Dani smiled back, her heart strangely light.

Josh draped his jacket over the back of a chair and rolled his shirt sleeves elbow high. Dani laughed as she watched him tie a large white dishtowel around his waist, then with one hand crack the eggs and drop them into a frying pan. "You're going to love this—I make fantastic scrambled eggs!"

Dani knew he was trying to ease her fears and at the same time wipe out the past unpleasantness. "Well, then do your stuff—I'll pour the milk."

After her large dinner at the hotel and terrifying race down the mountain, Dani was surprised at her voracious appetite. Together, they consumed six eggs, four slices of toast, and a quart of milk. Not until they had finished and sighed with contentment, did they begin to speak of the thoughts uppermost in both their minds.

Josh folded his arms across his chest and assumed an official tone. "It's not wise to go out alone at night—even in a National Park. It's as well patrolled as possible, but we can't be everywhere at once."

Dani nodded in agreement.

"Not long ago," he went on, "law enforcement was almost unnecessary. Today this place is a zoo. More and more of our interpretations rangers are training for law enforcement positions. Too bad. People leave the city to get away from crime, only to find it preceded them here."

He raked long fingers through his hair, then pulled at the edges of his mustache. "Don't go out at night without an escort again. Okay?" The concern in his eyes touched her, and she wondered if his words were personal or general.

Confusion tied her thoughts in knots. Why would anyone blackmail this man? Could Joshua possibly be guilty of anything worthy of Mark's interest? What about the clothes? The wife? Dani shook her head to clear her mind. She changed the subject. "Josh, do you think Edna is improving as quickly as she ought?"

"What do you mean?"

"It's just that she seems to be taking more nitro-glycerin now than when I first arrived."

"I didn't know that. I'll talk to her about it."

"Wouldn't she be better off in a convalescent home with professional care?"

"That's why I hired you." His brows drew together almost touching. "I wouldn't subject her to a home. She'd die there—just give up and die."

"I can't picture Edna as the type who'd give up over anything."

Josh smiled. "You're referring to her faith, aren't you? That's what keeps her going. And you're probably right. She'd very likely make a convalescent home her mission field and go about converting all the wheelchair patients." He chuckled and his eyes twinkled under thick lashes.

Dani smiled at the thought. "I know she loves being here with you. You're her life."

"She's quite a woman. Always stood by me when I was in trouble. The least I can do now is stand by her."

"Haven't you any other brothers or sisters?"

"No. There was an older sister, but she died when I was three years old. I guess I kept Mother busy enough, though. I understand I was quite a handful." Josh's boyish grin tugged at Dani's heart, and she could imagine what a loveable child he must have been.

"No aunts or uncles or grandparents?" she continued to question, hoping to learn more while he was in a talkative mood.

"Oh, a couple of distant cousins, I think. How about you?"

"Only child. Spoiled rotten, I guess—"

"That's hard to believe," he interrupted. "I've watched you care for Mother, and even though I didn't approve of your going off to Fresno that way, Mother told me she wanted you to go. She really likes you, you know." He reached across the table and covered her hand with his. "She seems to think you and I have a lot in common. I guess as far as she's concerned, we're both a couple of backsliders who need to come back to the Lord."

Dani felt the warmth of the large hand spread through her body and redden her face. She drew her hand away and laced her fingers together in front of her. After several moments, she spoke. "We may have a few things in common, but as you know, I am already interested in someone else."

Her heart pounded in her ears as she forced herself

to draw back. She couldn't become involved with Joshua Talbott—not if she were expected to spy on him. She held her breath as Josh stared at her, obviously trying to understand her change in attitude.

When he spoke it was in a light-mannered tone. "Don't get me wrong, Dani. I'm not interested in an involvement with you, either. A woman just wouldn't fit into my life right now."

"But how about those women's clothes?" The words tumbled out before she could stop them. She clapped her hand over her mouth, and stared wide-eyed as she watched the blood rush to Josh's face, bulging in large veins at his temples.

"I wondered when you'd get around to that. And now that you've admitted you were snooping in my closet, I could aim a few questions your way." He inhaled deeply, then spoke in a controlled voice, "But I'd prefer to remember this interlude as a pleasant one in our short acquaintance. I think it's time to say good-night."

With finality Josh pushed his chair back and stood up. His eyes brushed lightly over her as if to paint her image on the canvas of his memory, then bowing slightly, he picked up his jacket and strode from the room. A genuine "Lone Ranger." That's what Mark had called him.

When Dani fell exhausted into bed, she noticed that it was after four o'clock. Since Martha was still on duty, Dani looked forward to sleeping late. She tossed and turned a few times before settling on a comfortable position. Her last thoughts before drifting off to sleep were, *Tell them. Get your life right with God, then tell them. Give up this deception. No matter what the cost . . .*

The late morning sun peeked around the edges of the drapes, sketching yellow stripes across Dani's 'bed. She lifted her head and opened heavy eyelids to see that it was eleven o'clock. She had practically slept the entire morning away.

Cocking her head toward the door, she could hear Edna and Martha talking quietly in the kitchen. Was Josh still asleep? She hugged herself as she thought of the pleasant time they had shared the night before—at least until she opened her big mouth and crammed her foot in.

After a quick shower, she dressed casually in jeans and a pink polo shirt. After wearing her silk dress home last night, Dani knew it would be useless to continue her Plain-Jane disguise in front of Josh. She brushed her hair back and fastened it into a long ponytail, then tied it up with a piece of bright pink yarn. A dab of rosy lipstick, a touch of mascara, and she was ready to face Joshua Talbott and his mother with the truth. Her job wasn't as important to her as these people. A clear conscience would feel good, too.

"Well, well, here comes the sleepyhead," Edna drawled. "Joshua told us that you showed up late last night. I'm sorry your meeting didn't work out, dear."

"Oh, I think it was for the best," Dani said, bouncing into the room and sidling up close to Edna on the sofa. "You know what they say about all things working out."

Edna smiled and patted the Bible in her lap. "I guess you're thinking of Romans, chapter eight, verse twenty-eight. It says, 'And we know that in all things God works for the good of those who love him, who have been called according to his purpose.'"

"Do you really believe that?" Dani asked, thinking of the events that had taken place in her own life lately—the deceptions, the misunderstandings, the chase down the mountain.

"I certainly do," she said, without wavering. "My

confidence in a sovereign, loving Father is what makes life worth living."

Dani patted the thin hand. "Then why do you believe you had a heart attack? What good did it do?"

"Well, my dear, of course I don't have all the answers now, but I know a few of them." Edna counted on her fingers. "Because of my illness, I'm here with my son instead of alone in an apartment in Sacramento. I can see what hurts him, and what a great responsibility he has here. And because of what I see, I pray. I pray he'll remember the Lord who loves him, and begin to trust God with details much too big for one man. And," she added, "I would never have met you. You're as dear to me as a daughter. Not at all like Marlena—" She stopped midsentence, and blinked. "Please don't tell Josh I mentioned her."

"Of course, you have my promise—but who is Marlena?" It was personal curiosity that prompted Dani to ask. *No* more spying for her.

"I shouldn't tell you, but, well, Marlena was Joshua's wife."

Dani's chest ached, and a large lump filled her throat.

"She and Josh were only married one year when she was killed."

"I'm so sorry. I didn't know."

"No one here knows, except Betty and Bill McCall, of course. They've been Joshua's friends since school days. Went their separate ways for several years, but I think he confides in them sometimes. Even a man needs that, you know."

Dani began to understand why she had seen Josh with Betty that night at Mirror Lake. At least it seemed more reasonable than her first theory. And those clothes—Marlena's? But why had he kept them so long? Dani's voice was soft. "He must have been heartbroken. She was killed?"

"I mustn't talk about it anymore. Of course, I trust you dear, but there's much more involved, and there was ugly publicity at the time. Joshua has borne a great deal of grief these past few years, but now here, far away from the past, he's finding a new life for himself." She smiled coyly at Dani. "I was hoping you'd be part of that new life."

Dani flushed, and to change the subject, asked, "By the way, where is that son of yours? It's almost lunchtime, and I haven't seen hide nor hair of him. Is he out in the field today?"

"No, as a matter of fact, this morning he was called away on an emergency. He said he'd be gone for at least a week, and that he knew he could trust you to take good care of things here."

As Dani turned this latest news over in her mind, Martha called them to lunch. Her confession would have to wait until Josh came back. He would have to be told first, then decide if Edna could bear to hear that her companion was really a researcher trying to expose the chief ranger and the National Park Service.

Dani used Joshua Talbott's absence as an opportunity to get acquainted with the other rangers. Edna insisted she get out for some relaxation when she took her afternoon naps, and Dani either headed for the Visitors' Center to chat with rangers, or she wandered through the other buildings on the common, watching and listening to comments of both rangers and tourists. She had given up on her idea to search Joshua's office now that she had reached a decision to confess her purpose in coming to Yosemite, but her interest in park management and the people involved still intrigued her. So far, all she had learned about the chief ranger was that he was deeply respected as a man who not only knew his business, but carried it out with the highest regard for the wilderness, for the people who came to enjoy the park, and for the National Park Service.

Knowing that Mark spent his Saturdays in the office, Dani finally decided to call him.

"So you're still on the job," he said, a note of sarcasm in his voice. "After you ran out on me, I thought you may have skipped the country—but Bridges assured me he'd seen you several times."

The mention of Bridges' name clouded the bright day, but Dani replied calmly, "I haven't seen him, but I assure you, I'm still here."

"Well, I did expect to hear from you before now. Your note implied that this fantastic idea of yours would produce the evidence we need to start the wheels of the printing press rolling." He chuckled, then continued, "I was disappointed that you left Wawona. In fact, I thought seriously of calling you back to the city and scrapping the park exposé entirely."

"Well, that might not be a bad idea. So far I haven't had much success. I wasn't able to get into Talbott's office as I'd planned, and the guy, as far as I can see, is Mr. Clean."

"How about the women's clothes? And is there any more information about the wife?"

Dani glanced at her watch, and realized that it was time for her to get back. "I have to leave now. Edna is due to wake from her nap—and I feel especially responsible with Josh gone."

"Talbott's gone? This should be a perfect time for you to do some snooping around. We need some answers. Soon." Mark paused, then said with finality, "One month, Dani, that's all I can give you now. If we don't have something substantial by then, I'll have to make other plans."

As Dani trudged back up the hill, she breathed a sigh of relief. She only needed to stall a little longer, and she'd be off the hook. Edna would be well enough to no longer need a companion, and Mark would let this probing into Josh's life fall by the wayside, and Josh—what about him? Would he forget her? Could she forget him?

She inhaled the rich fragrance of the overhanging boughs. In such a short time she had come to love this beautiful valley, and now she would have to leave. The "Incomparable Valley" had been rightly named. Her eyes picked out the brilliant splotches of color, ranging from pale yellows to gold oranges, on the path before her, and she glowed under the narrow rays of afternoon sun playing through the branches. Bluejays squawked their greeting, and chipmunks scurried to hide in the ferns bordering the road.

Dani lifted her head and scanned the high cliffs that hovered over the valley. What a thrill those first white men must have felt when they discovered Yosemite Valley. It thrilled her every time she stepped out the front door. It was like walking into a great cathedral— into the presence of God.

"Have a nice walk?" Edna sat on the porch holding a flower in her hand. "You looked mighty deep in thought."

"I was." Dani flashed a bright smile. "I'm getting caught up in this place. I don't know if I'll be able to leave."

"Who says you're leaving?" Edna's usually smooth forehead creased in a frown.

"No one yet, but," Dani said, pointing her finger at Edna, "just look at you. You're getting so healthy, you'll soon be looking after me!"

"I have a feeling you do quite well looking after yourself." Edna smiled, then as an afterthought, she said, "I might be able to encourage you in your spiritual life, though." She nodded her head. "Yes, in fact, how about the two of us attending church tomorrow morning?"

"I'd like that Edna, really." She was surprised at her own quick response. She did want to go to church with Edna.

"Good. We'll go to the village chapel."

Dani thought of the many times she had passed the little chapel and admired it. The brown frame building with yellow trim was situated off the south road and surrounded by fruit trees as well as oak and elm. It reminded her of the New England churches she had visited as a child. "Yes, Edna, I'm looking forward to it."

The next morning, Dani was ready early and helped Edna dress for the Sunday service. Ministers from several denominations conducted their meetings at different times, and they had decided on one listed as interdenominational. At eleven o'clock, the service began. Dani felt mildly nervous. It had been several years since she had been to church to worship. Since moving to San Francisco, she had been in a church only to attend two weddings and a funeral. But since meeting Edna, and having time to sort out her own values, her heart longed to pray, to sing, to worship with other Christians.

As they walked through the doors of the small building, Dani glanced around at the people seated on wooden pews. Not many had come from the campgrounds and cabins to worship, but those present appeared lively and interested in their surroundings. A seat toward the front attracted Edna's eye, and Dani followed her up the aisle, all the while self-conscious of the clicking of her heels against the floorboards. They had been seated only a few minutes when a young woman stepped to the platform and with a wide smile announced, "Let's sing a few choruses. We'll begin with 'God Is So Good,' then 'Seek Ye First the Kingdom of God,' and we'll end with 'His Name Is Wonderful.' "

The congregation of about thirty people lifted their voices in song as the woman accompanied them with a guitar. As Dani sang, her nerves calmed and she began to concentrate on the words. Several times her eyes met Edna's, and she sensed the oneness they experienced through their joint worship. After the pastor—a young man who introduced himself as a Bible college student—prayed, Edna opened her Bible, and Dani followed along with the Scripture reading. Memories of Sunday school picnics, family potlucks, and New Year's services intruded upon her thoughts. Those had been happy days. She had wanted to go to church. All of her friends attended, and her first boyfriend was a classmate she had led to the Lord. There were always enough activities to provide a full social life and meet her needs for fun and companionship. Then she went away to college.

Her friends changed. Her family changed. Her church changed. Or was she the one who had changed? "And so friends . . ." The pastor's voice softened as he concluded the message. "Let us remember the words of the Lord Jesus Christ when he spoke to Martha, 'But one thing is needful; and Mary hath chosen that good part, which shall not be taken away from her.' Choose the eternal, folks. Choose God's way. Don't pile up a life of regrets; live each day to the fullest with Christ as your Lord."

Those last words tapped a rhythm as the congregation stood to sing the closing hymn—"Choose the eternal; choose God's way." Yes, that was the answer. She needed to renew her choice, to walk again with the Lord. She'd have to think about that for a while, though. Edna looped her arm through Dani's, and the two walked out of the dim light into a brilliantly clear Sunday.

The rest of the afternoon was spent in reading and resting. Dani felt happy with the new awareness of

God's touch on her life, but she was hesitant to share her feelings with anyone—even Edna. So many plans she had made didn't include God, and most of them were of great importance to her. She wanted to succeed in her position at Westcoast Publishing Company, advance to an editor's job, and eventually move on to a larger, more successful firm. And there was Mark Hutchinson. At one time, she had fantasized a romantic involvement with him, but his kiss at the Wawona had left her feeling used and cheap. He wasn't really what she wanted in a man. Now Joshua Talbott . . .

She hadn't planned on the feelings he aroused. His touch, his glance, even the sound of his voice affected her in a way that was new and foreign. Ridiculous. She didn't want to be in love with a park ranger. She was a city girl, sophisticated and . . .

Edna's voice from the living room interrupted her daydreams. "Dani, Josh is here. I heard his car. Come out on the porch with me!"

Dani's heart began to pound out of control. She smoothed her long hair into place and touched her face with her palms. She licked her lips, took a deep breath, and walked as casually as possible to the front door. "What did you say, Edna?"

"I said Josh is . . ." Edna's words froze in her throat.

Josh wasn't alone. A tall brunette, her arm linked through his, matched his stride up the walk. She glanced sidelong at Dani, then fastened her eyes on the other woman. "Well, Edna, Joshua and I have a wonderful surprise for you—we're going to be married!"

CHAPTER 6

DANI'S HEAD BEGAN TO SPIN. Josh—married? She wasn't sure who was supporting whom as Edna took her arm to follow the couple into the house.

"Edna, my dear, it's so good to see you again," the brunette drawled. "Joshua has told me all about your heart attack, and I'm so glad I can be with you in your time of recovery."

She batted her eyelashes at Josh, ignoring Dani's presence. "Our Joshua," she added, "helped me through my long convalescence, and now I'm here to help you through yours."

"It's a . . . a surprise to see you again, Amanda. You look quite well." Edna sat stiff-backed on the sofa, her hand still on Dani's arm. "But as you see, I already have help." She patted Dani's hand and shrugged her shoulders in apology. "We've been quite rude—Dani Fuller, this is Amanda Jennings."

Dani nodded at Amanda, who barely glanced her way. "Josh," Edna went on, directing crisp words to her son, who squirmed uneasily, "I do wish you would explain what's going on. I will say . . ." She inhaled deeply. "You've certainly handed me a surprise."

Joshua Talbott stood awkwardly in the center of the room looking down on Dani while Amanda looped her arm through his and tipped her chin. "Yes, Joshua, I think Edna does deserve an explanation. You naughty boy, surprising her like that. You should have told her of our plans to be married."

Josh's heavy eyebrows waggled and he cleared his throat. "Well, we can talk about it later. Right now, I'll bring your bags in." He released himself from her grasp and strode out of the room.

Amanda slinked over to the sofa. "Danny? How quaint. I've never heard a woman called Danny before." Her green eyes were cold and appraising.

"It's Danielle." She stared back at the tall woman, her eyes shooting the same icy sparks.

Edna interrupted the cool silence. "Dani is a nurse. She's been here for about a month now, and plans to stay at least through the summer. Longer if I can arrange it."

Dani thought Edna looked extremely pale as she watched her slip a tiny pill under her tongue.

"I'll stay as long as you need me," she said, placing her hand on the woman's knee.

"You won't be needed much longer. Joshua and I plan to be married as soon as possible. And I'm perfectly capable of caring for Edna. Besides, we've known each other a long, long time." Amanda reached down to pat Edna's head. "Haven't we, dear?"

"Dani, I hoped Josh would explain—Amanda is, I mean, was, Marlena's half-sister. She is Josh's former sister-in-law."

"Already an honorary member of the family," Amanda announced. "And now I'm to be a full-fledged Talbott." She swept her gaze over the elegantly furnished room. "I'd almost forgotten what beautiful things Marlena had."

Before she could continue, she saw Josh cross the room loaded down with bags and quickly followed him to the small guest room under the stairs.

Dani and Edna stared after them, then at each other. Neither spoke, but as if reading her mind, Edna suggested, "Why don't you get out for a breath of fresh air? I think I need to lie down for a while. This has come as quite a shock to me."

The older woman shook her head in disbelief. "It's so unlike him. There's more to this than meets the eye." She smiled at Dani. "I'm sure he has a plausible explanation."

Dani watched Edna's shoulders slump, and felt a lump form in her throat. Quickly she trotted through the living room, banging the front door. Down the steps. Away from the house. Sights and sounds blurred into each other as she ran down the hill, past the village, and up the path to the falls. She raced past the many tourists gazing upward—the fine mist spraying on their faces. Her feet took her up the path, over rocks and boulders, slipping, sliding, until she reached the base of Yosemite Falls where the roar drowned out her sobs. The water washed salty tears from her eyes. *Josh engaged.* Why had she dared to dream that maybe, someday—what a fool she'd been! Until now she hadn't been able to admit what she was feeling for Joshua Talbott, and now it was already over. But then, had he ever noticed her?

She had sensed something between them the night before he left. For once they had been able to talk, discovering mutual interests in music and literature. Then there was that long gaze before he said goodnight. She trembled, remembering the strength of his arms and his pounding heart as he held her after her scare.

Amanda Jennings. She was so unlike Josh. Brassy and artificial. What did he see in her? What had she meant when she said Josh helped her in her convalescence?

Dani forged on up the trail, oblivious to the darkening skies. She'd always wanted to climb to the top of the falls. Today it would feel good to expend her energy, to climb until she was numb.

Out of breath and drenched with the cold spray, she stopped and perched herself on the edge of a black boulder. The top was much farther than she could go so late in the day; she would rest a few minutes before starting back down. Edna would miss her being nearby.

The view below was spectacular. From her vantage point, she could see down the valley where Half Dome jutted into the evening sky. Cathedral Rocks hovered across the meadow, and once again Dani thought how like heaven this place must be. Heaven. Was it only this morning that she had gone to church and felt God's love warming her heart?

She glanced down at her clothes. The wet pink shirt clung to her body, emphasizing every curve and shadow, and she was glad for the gathering darkness. She should start back. She didn't want to worry Edna. Joshua's mother had already taken one nitroglycerin tablet today.

No other hikers were on the path, and Dani thought it seemed steeper going down than it had climbing up. Her shoes slipped on the rocks and she scratched her hands where she reached out to catch herself. Finally, at the bottom, she sat on the bench where she had viewed the falls on the day of her arrival. How differently she felt now. Her job was in jeopardy. She had deceived someone she cared for, and to top it all, the one man who stirred her heart was engaged. Where was God, anyway?

"Dani." A low voice startled her, and as she realized its owner, she began to shake. "I thought you might come here." Josh pulled off his sweater and wrapped it around her shoulders. "You're soaked. Have you been up the trail?" His eyes were soft, so soft and gentle, and as they searched her face, Dani felt weak. With his hands still on her shoulders, he pulled her toward him. "Dani, I have to talk to you."

"How about Amanda? Aren't you afraid she'll disapprove?"

"Dani, please," he groaned, tightening his grip on her shoulders. "Please come to my car where you'll be warm. I want to explain."

"You owe me no explanation, Mr. Talbott. I'm only the hired help. It's your mother who needs an explanation."

"Please?"

Dani reluctantly followed Josh down the path to where he had parked his car at the side of the road. "I always keep some dry clothes in the backseat. Why don't you change into them so you won't catch cold."

"Here?" She tried to imagine herself wriggling out of wet shirt and jeans into the gray sweats he held out to her. "I think we'd better go home."

"No. Mother is resting now, and Amanda is . . . well, she's doing something in her room." Josh's voice was firm. "I want you to change—now. I won't look."

In the darkness of the backseat, Dani struggled out of her wet clothes and into the oversized fleecy ones as Josh sat behind the wheel, his eyes straight ahead. "I've spoken to Mother about this 'surprise,' and she insisted I talk to you."

"Oh." Dani felt disappointed. "I thought it was your idea."

"Well, I did want to tell you about Amanda the night before I left, but . . ." He paused as she climbed into the front seat. "I didn't want to ruin the good time we were having."

"Did you have a good time, too?" She leaned toward him, feeling a rush of warmth flow into her body and up to her face. "I guess that's the only time we've been alone." Dani's voice drifted off.

A smile tugged at Josh's lips and rearranged his mustache before he started the engine. "Let's go somewhere else. Are you warm now?"

"Oh, yes. I feel much better." Once again a sense of hope rose in her heart. But why? Joshua Talbott was engaged, and she knew him to be a loyal man, not only as a dedicated ranger, but to his own word.

The silence stretched between them as Josh drove down the narrow road to Mirror Lake. Dani wondered if he always brought women to this place. She glanced at him and saw his teeth flash a smile in the darkness.

"You've been here at night before, haven't you, Dani? I know you were here the night I found you going through my closet."

A twinge of fear darted up her spine, but she smiled and raised her right hand. "I plead the fifth!"

"I'm not sure what you heard that night, or why you were here, but I had come to talk to Betty about the situation I'd gotten myself into, and . . ." He sighed. "Here I am, going over the same thing again."

Josh opened her door and held out his hand. His long fingers wrapped around hers brought a fluttering weakness to her stomach, but she tried to sound calm. "You're lucky to have so many confidantes."

Still holding her hand, he led her to the water's edge. Only a sliver of a crescent moon smiled on the black satin of the lake, and together, they stood silently enjoying the glassy beauty. Dani wished the moment could last forever. Josh's large hand felt so warm, so protective around hers, and his tall form beside her gave the feeling that all was well after all.

She glanced up at him. In the pale moonlight, she could trace the perfect outline of his straight nose and high forehead. The strong smooth chin jutted out stubbornly, and he turned toward her, dropping her hand. Then placing both hands on her face, he tilted it toward his. Her heart pounded fiercely, and she felt she would faint. She waited quietly as the gentle night air washed over them and the stars twinkled in the vast blackness overhead. He was standing so close that she could feel the warmth of his breath on her forehead.

"Dani . . ." His hand warmed the back of her neck, and his voice cracked, "If only . . ."

He didn't finish his sentence, but brushed his lips over her forehead, then rested them lightly on each closed eyelid, and at last, gently, softly, his lips touched hers, first curiously tender, then wonderfully possessive. Her hands moved up his broad chest to rest on the back of his neck as she surrendered herself to his embrace. His arms tightened about her. His lips, soft and hungry, consumed her, and she forgot about everything else.

"I'm sorry. I didn't mean for this to happen." He stepped back.

Josh's words jolted her back to reality. In the darkness, she could see his eyes filling themselves with every part of her face, her hair, before he turned and leaned against a moss-covered rock. "I don't want to hurt you. There can never be anything between us."

"But there already is something between us—I love you!" She could hardly believe her own ears. Had she said, "I love you?"

Dani's large eyes shone through tears, and her small face looked even smaller as her full hair tumbled over the heavy fleece shirt. She seemed lost in the oversized clothes, and Josh leaned toward her, then

87

stopped himself. He touched her lips with a forefinger. "No, don't say it. You're young and vulnerable, and I took advantage of you."

He raked his fingers through his hair and rested against the rock, crossing one leg over the other. "I'm engaged to Amanda and had no right. I'm sorry."

She didn't know what to say. She wasn't sorry for the kiss, but—now what?

Dani lifted her chin and pushed her hair behind her shoulders. Her heart ached for the pain she saw etched on Josh's strong face, but she said nothing.

"If you want me to take you home now, I will."

"But you brought me here to talk. About Amanda? About my leaving? What do you want to say?" She thought she sounded quite controlled and calm.

"I owe you an explanation, now more than ever." He touched her shoulder, allowing his fingers to linger longer than necessary. "Come on, let's sit down at the edge of the lake. This will take a while. I want you to understand my position."

He pulled some long grasses down for them to sit on and gazed out over the water. "I love it here, and yet I think I'll have to leave soon."

"But why?"

"Please, just let me talk. You'll understand in a few minutes, and it's hard for me to face all this again." His voice trembled, and he reached into his pocket for a handkerchief. After he blew his nose, he continued, "Marlena and I were married for only a year when she was killed in an auto accident. Amanda was in the car, too, and was in critical condition for months. In the past two years, she's been undergoing physical therapy as well as psychiatric care."

He glanced toward her, his face drawn and haggard. Dani nodded her understanding.

"I've felt responsible for Amanda, and still do. I saved all of Marlena's possessions for Amanda, even Marlena's clothes."

Dani interrupted, "But she's well now. Why should you feel so responsible?"

Josh's eyes closed and Dani could see a tear ooze from the corner of his eye and glide down his nose.

"Because . . . I drove the car that killed my wife and injured her sister!"

Dani was numb. It all fit together. The secrecy. The publicity Edna had spoken of.

Josh's voice rose. "I was not only accused of negligence, but the possibility of murder was splashed across the front page of the *Seattle News*. Marlena was quite wealthy, and we didn't get along from the first."

"Oh, Josh. I'm so sorry."

"I was cleared of those charges, but Amanda's attorney has been bleeding me for the hospital costs ever since. Not that I minded. I wanted to take care of her, but now she's threatened—she's threatened suicide if I don't marry her. She says I owe her."

Josh dropped his head in his hands, and Dani had an almost uncontrollable urge to cradle his head in her arms, but waited for him to go on.

"She's sick, Dani. I believe she'd do it. I can't have that on my conscience, too."

"Oh, Josh." It was all she could say. What a predicament. Wouldn't Mark just love to get ahold of that kind of information. She had to see that he didn't!

Josh lifted his head, his eyes searching the heavens for an answer. "I thought I was free from the past— with Amanda well, at least well enough to live on her own again, and the memories of Marlena fading—I have a new life here in the valley, and," he said, covering her hand with his, "then you came along."

He shrugged his shoulders and started to stand. "Well, I've unburdened my troubles on your shoulders. I don't know why, considering—but I trust you. And you know how Mother feels about you."

"Yes, I know, but I've already decided to leave."
Dani stood and began walking toward the car. "Since
Amanda is here to care for Edna, there's no need for
me to stay." She turned to glance over her shoulder.
"Especially after tonight, I'd feel very uncomfort-
able."

"Would you wait a while longer before you say
anything about leaving?" Josh's eyes pleaded with
her. "I knew this announcement would upset Mother,
but I think your being here will help her to make the
adjustment."

The ride home was quiet with both of them wrapped
in their own thoughts. As Dani opened the car door to
leave, she said, "I'll stay on and care for Edna until
you think she's well enough for me to leave, but until
then, I'll try to stay out of Amanda's way—and
yours. As for the episode at the lake, you were
probably right. We were both vulnerable." With those
words she slipped away from the car and around the
side of the house through the back door.

Several nights later, as Dani sat on the front porch
talking with Edna, Amanda stepped through the door
with a regal air. Her white shorts accentuated long
slender legs and a red tank top showed off her slim
angular body. She had combed her short dark hair
behind her ears, drawing attention to a flawless
complexion and large green eyes. She was a striking
woman, and Dani felt short and girlish in her presence. Not wanting to come between Edna and her
future daughter-in-law, Dani excused herself.

"Of course, Danny," Amanda said, stressing the
name as she would a curse. "Edna and I have many
things to talk about. Besides, Joshua will be home
soon, and I noticed you two don't get along."

Each day had been more unbearable than the day
before. She was more determined than ever to leave

as soon as possible. The friction could be of no help to Edna, and after Josh's kiss, Dani couldn't look at him without blushing. As she sat at the kitchen table drinking a glass of milk and trying to decide just how to tell Edna she was leaving, the older woman walked through the door. "I thought you might be in here. Please don't let Amanda get to you, dear."

"Oh, she didn't. I'm a little tired, that's all. Would you like me to get you something to eat?"

Edna shook her head, then sat down and leaned toward Dani. "Josh told me about Amanda's threats, and I don't believe for a minute that she'd carry them out." She smiled broadly and lifted her eyes. "And I don't believe my heavenly Father will allow my son to go through with this marriage."

She touched the end of Dani's nose in a playful manner. "I think he has someone else in mind for Josh."

She rose slowly from the chair and sighed. "I'm so very tired, too. Maybe a good night's rest will help both of us."

As Dani watched her shuffle slowly out of the room, she felt alarmed. Edna was ill. Her pallor was gray and her eyes too shiny. She folded her arms on the table and dropped her head. *Oh, dear God, please do something!*

"So here you are." Amanda's drawl broke through her concern. "I think we need to talk—now."

"We've nothing to talk about." Dani's voice was firm as she leaned back and met Amanda's glacial stare.

"Oh, you're mistaken." Amanda poured a cup of coffee and sat down opposite Dani, glaring over the rim of the cup. "As a matter of fact, we seem to have a mutual acquaintance."

Dani circled the edge of her glass with a forefinger. "If you're talking about Josh, I'm no threat to you there, Amanda."

"Oh, I know that, little girl. Joshua needs a woman, not a child. I have him all wrapped up. No, I was talking about someone else—someone who called me in Seattle to say I'd better get down here before a certain little *researcher* balls up the works!"

Dani's eyes flew open, and she struggled to speak around the lump in her throat. "Who? What are you talking about?"

"Now you want to talk to me, huh? I see I've been given the right information." Amanda's expression revealed her pleasure at Dani's discomfort, and she prolonged the agony by slowly sipping her coffee before continuing. "A certain man I know is also a friend of yours, Goody-Two-Shoes."

An icy pain ripped through Dani's chest, leaving her weak and shaken. "Ken Bridges?"

"Yes, Ken Bridges. He's told me all about you, sweetie—all about your plan to smear our great and mighty 'Lone Ranger' and his dear helpless little mother."

"It's not true. I—"

"You don't need to deny it, Miss Fuller. I've verified his story, and only wanted to confirm it before I break the news to poor old Edna and her darling son."

Dani felt the blood pounding in her temples. "You're evil. You don't love Josh, and you don't love Edna. Just what are you after? And why should you have anything to do with Ken Bridges?"

"Oh, so now *I'm* on trial. I think *you're* the one who has to give some answers. After all, Joshua and Edna know me. I'm Marlena's half-sister. I deserve to share in her inheritance—which I plan to do, one way or another."

"You don't scare me one bit, Amanda, but I don't want to hurt Edna, so I'll tell you why I'm here."

Amanda sucked in her cheeks and slanted her eyes at Dani. "Go ahead—let's hear your story."

"You're right . . . in part. I did come here to check out Joshua Talbott. I work for a small publishing company, and my boss is interested in doing an exposé on the National Park Service and its employees. Anyway," she groaned, "I didn't expect to find such a lovely person as Edna. I really do love her and can't hurt her. And as for Josh . . . Well, I don't think he's doing anything illegal or worthy of an exposé. Besides, I like him and wouldn't betray him, either."

"You love him, you mean!"

Dani winced at her statement, then replied softly, "Yes, I do. I do love Josh, but—"

"But he's going to marry me—and we're going to live happily ever after on all that money Marlena left him."

"That's it, isn't it? You're not sick and you have no intention of committing suicide. You're just using Josh's sympathy and grief to further your own greed."

"He owes me," Amanda cried. She pulled back her bangs to reveal a tiny scar on her forehead. Her voice rose hysterically. "Yes, my little Miss Fuller. I'm going to marry Joshua Talbott for his money, and not you or anyone else is going to stop me."

A gasp from the corner of the room caught their attention. Edna, her face white and drawn, clutched her chest and sank to the floor.

CHAPTER 7

EDNA'S EYES FLUTTERED OPEN to see Dani bent over her. "I'm all right, dear. But you'd better call the doctor."

"The number's on the wall beside the phone," Dani shot at Amanda. "Tell them to send an ambulance—then call Park Headquarters and get Josh here."

Amanda ran to the phone, her face white and her hands trembling.

"Are you in much pain?" Dani slipped a pillow under Edna's head and draped a light blanket over her.

"My chest feels so heavy—and—my arms are numb."

"Okay, dear. Don't talk, just try to breathe easily. Help is on the way."

Edna looked terrible—her skin was pale and clammy, and her eyes rolled back in her head. Her mouth drooped open grotesquely as she tried to get more air into her lungs.

Long minutes passed before three husky men

bustled into the kitchen and took their places around Edna. Dani and Amanda stood aside, watching in amazement as the medic in charge inserted an IV in Edna's hand, attached oxygen to her nose and taped small wires to her arms, chest, and ankles. After several tense moments, he looked up and announced, "She's had a heart attack, all right. We'll take her into Mariposa Community—they're expecting her." He gestured toward the two women. "You can ride with her if you want."

"Oh, no. I couldn't do that," Amanda blurted.

"Yes, I'll go." Dani's tone was decisive. "And her son will be here any minute. He'll go, too."

"Well, if Joshua is riding in the ambulance, so am I," Amanda's voice whined and she edged closer to the gurney where Edna lay, still and white.

"No time for argument," the man said, wheeling Edna to the waiting ambulance. "We've got to get her in there right now."

As they reached the ambulance, Josh skidded to a stop and flew out of the park truck. "Mother!" He glanced first at Dani, then at the medic. "Is she . . . ?"

"She's had a heart attack but seems stable right now. We're taking her into Mariposa."

"Good. Okay if I ride along?"

"Yes. The young lady is going, too." He motioned toward Dani.

Amanda looped her arm through Josh's and looked up into his frown-creased face. "But Joshua, I should be with you. Don't forget about me."

"Oh, for heaven's sake, Amanda. Think of some-one else for a change." He pointed toward the truck. "Here, take my keys and follow us. We'll need a way to get home." Josh didn't wait for an answer but gently placed his hand on Dani's back, nudging her into the ambulance, then climbed in beside her and leaned over his mother.

"You okay?" he whispered.

Edna nodded, her eyelids fluttering in recognition, then grimaced in pain. While the medics continued to monitor Edna's heart and administer drugs through the IV, Josh slipped his arm around Dani's shoulder and drew her close as if to gain strength.

The forty miles to Mariposa seemed like four hundred, and Dani turned over and over in her mind the incident that had preceded Edna's heart attack. Several times she started to tell Josh, but stopped. His present worry was enough. His arm about her was reassuring and although her concern for Edna superseded every other thought, she felt content.

Josh. Oh, Josh. Haven't you been through enough? She glanced down at his hand which gripped his knee. Such strong yet gentle hands. They seemed an extension of Joshua Talbott's essence. Courageous yet compassionate. Strong-willed yet serene. She had learned much about this ranger in a short time. Not what Mark had hoped she'd learn. Not what she'd expected when she agreed to take this job. She hadn't expected to fall in love, but how could she help it. Josh was all she had ever wanted in a man. He cared about people. Maybe too much, she thought, remembering his commitment to Amanda. He was the kind of man who took his relationships seriously. Her mind drifted back to the night of the car chase. They had both felt the love growing between them—and they had both pulled away. She didn't want to hurt him, and she knew he had a responsibility toward Amanda. H'm, life was certainly perplexing.

Dani sighed, and at the same moment, Josh turned toward her—a bond between them. They both loved Edna. They loved each other. Now what? Dani smiled, and at the same time touched the top of his hand with her fingertips. "She's going to be fine. I just know it. The Lord is with her."

97

"Yes." Josh's voice was husky. "I can feel his presence here. I know it, too."

The ambulance backed into a driveway leading to the emergency entrance, and immediately a crew of doctors and nurses took over. They whisked Edna off to another part of the hospital while Josh filled out forms and talked to the receptionist.

Dani watched him from the side of the room where she had slumped onto a faded green couch. His calmness and serenity in the situation renewed her confidence. Edna would be well again. She just couldn't die. *Oh, please God, don't let her die.*

Josh had finished admitting Edna and was walking toward Dani when Amanda suddenly burst into the room. "Well, I finally found you. I didn't even know where the hospital was—and I couldn't get the stupid truck started." She smoothed her hair and forced a smile. "Well, anyway I'm here now. Can we get a cup of coffee someplace?"

"No, I want to wait for the doctor's report." He looked at Dani. "Why don't you go get some coffee. You look tired."

Dani's face was strained and pale. "No, I'd rather wait here." She laced her fingers together in her lap and bit the edge of her lip. "He'll surely have some news for us soon."

"Well," Amanda said, nestling up to Josh and tracing his neck and shoulder with her forefinger, "then I guess I'll have to stay here and comfort my man."

Josh clenched his teeth, but said nothing. Dani wondered if he was just trying to ignore Amanda's remarks or if he didn't hear her. They sat opposite Dani on a matching drab green couch. It looked as though it would be a long wait, so Dani picked up a dog-eared magazine to absentmindedly leaf through its pages. Almost an hour passed before the doctor entered the waiting room. "Mr. Talbott?"

Josh jumped up from the couch and met the doctor halfway across the room.

"Your mother is doing fine. She's had another heart attack, but we've stabilized her and transferred her to Intensive Care. She's sedated and resting well, but if you'd like to see her, you may."

Josh followed the doctor down the hall and disappeared around the corner.

"Well, Danielle, I hope you're satisfied!" Amanda glared at her. "It's your fault Edna had that heart attack. It must have been quite a shock to hear that her precious little companion is really a spy." Her lip curled up in a sneer. "Now our wedding will have to be postponed until Joshua knows his *dear* mother is on the road to recovery."

"You don't even care about her, do you?"

"Well, let's say I'd be glad not to have to put up with a mother-in-law."

"You've got to be the most cold-blooded person I've ever known." Dani felt the blood rush to her face, and she reached to grasp Amanda's wrist. "I can't believe Josh could be deceived by you."

"Well, they say love is blind. I guess he just loves me so much he can't live without me. Why else would he keep Marlena's expensive clothes and her art collection? For me, of course."

"But he doesn't love you!"

"I suppose you think he loves you." Amanda jerked away from Dani's grip and folded her arms across her chest. "He loved Marlena and was responsible for her death . . . and my long convalescence. He may not love me, but I don't care. As long as he marries me, that's all that matters."

"He should know the kind of woman you are," Dani threatened.

"And I suppose you're the one to tell him? And hurt him again? I think you care about him more than that."

Dani's face paled as Amanda continued. "You've admitted you're in love with him, but you may just as well leave Yosemite and forget him. He's mine and I'll do everything in my power to keep him."

"You're not going to tell him about our conversation tonight, are you?" Dani hated the pleading tone of her voice, but she couldn't bear for Josh to know yet. She wanted to tell him herself at the right time.

"We'll just have to wait and see about that." Amanda stopped abruptly as Joshua Talbott strode back into the room, his face smooth and peaceful.

"She woke for a minute and told me to tell you not to worry, Dani. She understands. Whatever that means." He lifted his eyebrows in a question.

With a sigh of relief, Dani slumped back on the couch and closed her eyes. "Thank you, Lord," she murmured. "Thank you."

"I have to get back to the park," Josh said. "We can all go back for the night, then return in the morning."

"I'd rather stay here if it's all right with you." Dani dabbed at a tear that trickled down her cheek.

"Well, if you like." He paused in thought. "There's a motel across the street. Why don't you get a good night's sleep and I'll meet you back here in the morning." He pulled a small notebook from his shirt pocket and studied it. "I can get Bill McCall to check out those trails tomorrow, and then . . ." He slipped the book back into the pocket and grinned. "Then, Mother will no doubt have passed the crisis. I can think about what to do next when the time comes." He touched her arm with his fingertips. "Thanks, Dani. I appreciate all you've done for Mother. So does she."

Josh turned to leave when Amanda whined, "Don't forget me, Joshua Talbott. You act as if I'm not even here, and I'm your future wife." She lifted her chin in defiance. "You know how ill I've been. You should be more considerate."

"Sorry. I'm not thinking clearly." He shoved his hands into his pants pockets and ambled out the door with Amanda clinging to his arm. She said loud enough for Dani to hear, "Oh, Joshua, can I trust you all alone in that big, empty house?"

"You'd better believe it," he answered, letting the door swing shut behind them.

Several minutes passed before Dani glanced at her watch. She could hardly believe it was already midnight. No wonder she felt so weary. She stood up and stretched her arms and legs, then walked slowly down the darkened hallway to the nurses' station.

"Could I look in on Mrs. Talbott? She's in the ICU." Dani held her breath, waiting for an answer.

The buxom woman in white scanned a list of names on her clipboard before speaking. "Well, if you don't disturb the patient. I'm sure it will be all right if you just look in. She's on the second floor. I'll call up there to let them know you're coming."

It felt good to move about after sitting so long, and Dani walked past the elevator and pushed open the door marked "Stairs." Her footsteps echoed in the darkened stairwell, and she suddenly felt very much alone and afraid. Suppose Edna should die? Amanda would make sure Josh knew the cause of his mother's fatal attack. Oh, why did she ever let Mark talk her into taking this assignment? If only she'd stayed in San Francisco, content to pursue her career as a researcher in the office instead of fancying herself as a coauthor. What a fool she'd been.

She stepped into the quietness of the intensive care unit, punctuated only by the "blip-blip" of monitors and an occasional clank of a tray or bottle being moved. The odor of medication and the presence of death washed over her. A nurse motioned toward a curtained room, and Dani felt her heart tighten as she peered into the small cubicle. Edna lay so still, and the light from the nurses' station cast a gray pall over her face. Tubes seemed to be coming from everywhere, and with fascination, Dani watched the jagged line on the monitor measure the weakened heart rate.

"Is she . . . ?" Dani's voice rasped as she turned toward the nurse.

"She's doing fine." The young woman touched Dani's arm and smiled reassuringly. "She's a strong woman. Don't worry."

Without warning, a wave of grief washed over her, and she quickly excused herself and strode down the hall, breathing deeply to keep from crying. Edna would be all right. She had to be. She had so much to offer—her walk with the Lord was strong and her love for people showed through her every action.

As Dani descended the stairs to the waiting room, she reconsidered her doubts about coming to Yosemite. If she had stayed in San Francisco, she would never have known Edna—she had been such an inspiration. And then there was Josh. Even if there could never be anything between them, she was richer for having known him, for having touched him. Recalling his kiss revived that strange pounding in her heart, and she felt her face flush. Would there ever be anyone else for her?

Back in the waiting room, she decided not to check into the motel, but to curl up on the hard and worn sofa. At least she'd be near if there was a change in Edna's condition. The room was empty with only one nurse who bent over a stack of papers. Dani shoved a lumpy pillow this way and that before settling her head in its folds. She felt a heavy warmth of weariness cover her like a blanket. Her eyes closed against the dim light and she drifted into sleep.

She seemed to be slipping on a narrow, rocky path. A cold spray—was it from a waterfall?—sprinkled against her lashes, dimming her vision. A man approached, holding out his hands. Just as she reached for support, a voice broke through her consciousness. "Dani? Are you all right?"

Her eyes fluttered open to see a clean-shaven face bent over her. Gray eyes shone behind dark lashes. A waft of cigarette smoke tickled her nose. "Mark!"

Dani sat upright, confused, not knowing where she was. The smells and sounds of the hospital jolted her back to reality. Edna. Josh. What was Mark doing here?

"News travels fast," he said sitting beside her. "I was on my way up to see you and stopped to give you a call. A ranger told me about Mrs. Talbott." His voice was low and echoed concern. "How did it happen?"

"Oh, Mark. It was awful," she blurted, glad for a familiar face. "Amanda, that's Talbott's fiancée, knew all about me, about my job. Ken Bridges had told her everything. Edna overheard her."

"Hey, wait a minute. Slow down." Mark lit another cigarette and studied Dani's face. "Are you telling me that Bridges has had contact with Amanda Jennings?"

"You know about her?"

"Yes. In fact, when I didn't hear from you for several days, I called Ken. He told me about this Jennings woman and her relationship to Talbott." He rubbed his chin. "He didn't say anything about calling her though." A glint shone in his eyes as he inhaled on the cigarette and slowly let the smoke drift out of his mouth and nostrils. "I knew there was more to this ranger than meets the eye. An accident. A death. Another woman. Might be a good story after all."

"Oh, please Mark, let's forget it. There's been so much pain and hurt already. And now Edna. Can't we just scrap the whole idea?"

103

"Hey, listen little lady, I'm in business, remember?" He tipped her chin with his forefinger. "You're not too involved with these people, are you?"

She tried to swallow the giant lump that blocked her words. Instead, a river of tears streamed down her face and a sob escaped her lips. "Oh, yes, I'm involved. Edna is like a mother to me, and Josh . . . "

"So the charismatic 'Lone Ranger' has another notch on his belt, huh?"

"He's not like that." Her voice steadied and she glared at the man next to her. "He's only trying to do what's right by Amanda, and oh, you'd have to hear the whole story to understand."

"So why don't you tell me all about it." Mark leaned back and propped his feet in front of him on the low table covered with old magazines and chipped ashtrays. He draped his arm behind Dani on the back of the couch and waited for her to speak.

Should she tell him all she knew? Would it help him to understand why he shouldn't write a book about the chief ranger at Yosemite? Surely he had a conscience and wouldn't hurt innocent people.

The words tumbled out, one on top of the other, as she told about Amanda's unexpected arrival and the shock it had been to Edna. Without telling about her conversation with Josh at the lake, Dani let him think Edna had told her about the accident and Amanda's threat to take her own life. As she rambled on, Mark's arm came to rest around her shoulders, and in her weariness, she leaned her head against his chest. It was a relief to tell someone about the things that had been on her mind—someone she could be honest with—someone who knew her and why she was here.

"Dani," Mark said, his lips moving in her hair, "how about Talbott? What are your feelings for him? I get the distinct impression that you're not telling all."

"There's nothing more to tell," she said, lifting her face to his. "Josh is going to marry Amanda, and I'm coming back to San Francisco. If I still have a job?"

Mark's hand pressed against her shoulder, drawing her closer. "I'm sure we can work something out."

Dani turned her face away and leaned her head against his chest again. "Thanks, Mark. I really appreciate it. Maybe my next assignment will be more successful. Maybe . . ."

But she didn't finish her sentence. The events of the day had drained her of strength, and she settled against Mark and once more slipped into the darkness of slumber.

Once or twice throughout the night, Dani awoke realizing she was in Mark's arms, but not wanting to disturb him, she closed her eyes and tried to imagine a favorable outcome of the past months' events. Edna would get well, Josh and Amanda would be married, and she, what would she do? Go back to the city with Mark? He was obviously interested in her, but she believed it was only a conquest, not because he genuinely cared.

Fitful dreams punctuated by sirens and voices seemed to come and go whenever she turned her head or stretched her legs. Then as early morning light filtered through her eyelids, a harsh voice penetrated the restless dreaming.

"Well, Joshua, will you look at this. Seems our little nursie has found herself a man!"

It must be a nightmare. Dani closed her eyes tightly and nestled closer against Mark's cashmere sweater. Reality finally sank in, and she bolted to a sitting position. "Amanda! Josh?"

She stared first at the smirking woman above her, then blushing, looked from Josh's startled face to Mark's straight, even smile.

Mark lifted himself to stretch his shoulders and arms, smoothed his hair with his hand, all the while watching the couple in front of him as their eyes raked over Dani.

Dani brushed her hair back from her face and adjusted her blouse. She was clearly flustered and embarrassed, and her eyes pleaded with Josh for understanding, but his were cold and scrutinizing.

"We thought you'd be at the motel," he finally said.

"Maybe she was there." Amanda's whiny voice had an edge to it. "Is that where you found this handsome man?"

Dani's large blue eyes flashed. "Maybe you'd better mind your own business."

Deciding it was worthless to spar with Amanda, Dani turned to Josh. "This is the friend I told you about. The one I was to meet in Fresno. Mark Hutchinson, this is Joshua Talbott, my employer."

Her last words were emphatic, and Josh narrowed his eyes at her before taking Mark's outstretched hand.

Comparing the two men, Dani thought they couldn't be more opposite. Though both were tall and dark, Josh seemed stronger and more vibrant. Little muscles rippled in his forearm as he shook hands, and the hours of living in the outdoors had tanned his skin and filled his wavy hair with streaks of sunshine. Even his eyes seemed to have captured little glints of gold in their warm brown pools.

She inhaled deeply and pulled her eyes away to look at Mark. Natural olive skin, high cheekbones, jaw now showing the signs of a beard—Mark's good looks were out of place in this small mountain hospital. He belonged in the city, and as she glanced back at Josh's stern expression, she thought she would be better off in the city, too.

Amanda's voice interrupted her thoughts. "Joshua, I think Miss Fuller has something to tell you."

"What?" Dani felt her heart skip a beat. "What do you mean, Amanda?"

Her eyes narrowed as she nodded her head and continued to stare at Dani. "Don't you think Joshua should know that you're not what you claim to be?"

Now Josh's eyes narrowed and his jaws clenched. "Dani, what is all this about?"

"I think I can explain," Mark spoke up, but Dani placed her hand on his arm to silence him.

"No, Mr. Talbott deserves an explanation from me—the truth. Please sit down." Dani stirred her thoughts around in her mind, trying to decide where to begin. After a tense moment, she said calmly, "I'm not a registered nurse."

Josh's eyes widened, but she went on, "My resume was falsified, and I feel terrible. If I had been a nurse, I would have been able to help Edna. But . . ."

She swallowed deeply and looked at Josh with moist eyes. "I am sorry."

"But why? Why did you apply for a position as a companion? I specifically requested someone with nursing experience."

Dani expected that any minute Amanda would jump in with information about the research job, but she only sat quietly smirking, obviously saving it for another time. Well, Dani wasn't going to say any more, at least not now. Not in front of Amanda and Mark. She stared down at her hands folded together in her lap. The knuckles were white and the veins stood out like blue threads. They reminded her of the afghan Edna was crocheting.

Josh repeated, "Why, Dani? Why did you come up here?"

Mark's voice surprised her. "She needed a job, Talbott. It's as simple as that. And, well, she needed to get away from me." He slipped his arm around Dani's shoulder and looked down at her. "But now we've resolved our differences, and I hope she'll be coming back to the city."

She looked up into his face and joined in the act. "Yes, I guess I'll be returning soon. But," she said, her eyes pleading with Josh, "I would like to stay, at least until Edna is out of danger."

"Do you really care what happens to her?" Josh's tone was so cold, Dani had to repress a shiver. How could he think she didn't care?

"You know I do."

Now Josh's eyes betrayed a deep hurt, and he quickly turned his head and stood up, walking away from them. He seemed to be thinking, then turned again and stepped over to Dani. "I knew you were up to something, and I'm still not sure what, but don't blame yourself for Mother's condition. The doctor said another attack was inevitable. You made her happy while you were with her." He paused and tugged at his mustache before continuing. "And yes, I think you should stay, at least until we know what comes next. She'll want to see you. Unfortunately she's come to depend on you. So have . . ."

He stopped before finishing his sentence, and Dani felt the blood drain from her cheeks. Did he depend on her, too?

Now Amanda was next to him, her arm entwined through his. "Well, come along, darling. You wanted to see the doctor first thing this morning, and of course, we both want to see Edna." Instead of the whine, Amanda's voice had taken on the tone of confidence, and even her demeanor had changed. Her eyes sparkled with victory as she clung to Josh's arm, her long nails digging in, possessive as a cat's claws. She evidently felt sure of her position in Josh's life now, and the result was for the better.

108

He looked down at her, then again at Dani. The warmth in his eyes didn't match his words. "You'd better move your things out today. Maybe you can get a room at the lodge."

Dani felt as if she'd been slapped. "Yes, I'll do that."

"I've reserved a room at the Ahwahnee." Mark added quickly, "I'm sure you can get one there, too."

Josh's eyes lingered on her face a moment, then with a nod of his head he turned and walked away, his future wife keeping step with his long strides.

CHAPTER 8

SITTING BESIDE MARK in the comfort of his car, Dani was able to forget the conflicting pressures of the past weeks. As the road began to wind upward, the ranges of the High Sierra jabbed at the blue afternoon sky. Some of the faraway peaks seemed to be wearing cloud collars, and others still sported patches of snow in their deep crevasses.

"It's beautiful, isn't it?" Mark's voice broke through her thoughts. "I always enjoy coming up here."

"Yes, it is. I feel sad to be leaving."

"You knew when you took the assignment that you'd only be staying a couple of months."

Dani nodded before leaning her head against the cushions. "But at the time, Yosemite was only a green square on the map, not rugged cliffs, waterfalls, and lush meadows."

"Or Joshua and Edna Talbott."

Dani looked at the man beside her. He was more observant than she'd given him credit. He knew she had allowed herself to get involved with the Talbotts—something that was *verboten* for a good researcher. She'd brought all this heartache on herself. She wasn't a good researcher; she was weak and vulnerable. She was in love. She'd known it from the first time she saw Josh Talbott at the waterfall. It was stupid and unheard of—love at first sight—but that love had grown into a deep mature caring; so deep that she was willing to give him up.

"I'm sorry," Dani said softly. "I've been using that phrase a lot lately, but I am sorry. I wasn't 'enterprising' as you'd hoped. I haven't been objective or merciless." She paused, then said with finality, "And that's what it takes."

Mark covered her hand with his and took his eyes off the road to face her. "You're right about not being much of a researcher, but you're quite a woman!"

His words startled her, and she flushed under his penetrating gaze.

"Yes, Danielle Fuller, I much prefer you as a woman to a cold, official investigator. You keep doing what you're doing, whatever it is. I like it."

"But I really wanted to succeed as a researcher. I want to make a name for myself," she argued. "Anyone can be a 'woman.'" She stared out the window as they approached the entrance station to Yosemite National Park.

"Amanda is a woman," she declared, the bitterness seeping through her words.

"No," Mark said firmly. He flashed his Golden Eagle passport at the smiling young ranger and drove under the Arch Rock, following close behind a camper. "No, Amanda Jennings is only a caricature of a woman. She's phony, cheap, and totally without feeling."

"Well, you certainly sized her up in a hurry."

"That's my business—people. I make my living off their character flaws. Remember?"

"Oh, Mark, that sounds so deprecating. Don't talk that way about yourself."

"You mean you think there's some good in me? That I'm not a complete washout in your eyes?" A smile played at the corners of his mouth.

"You're just trying to get me to compliment you . . . and I will. I didn't thank you for jumping in to help me explain my falsified resume. I thought Amanda was going to tell Josh about my job at Westcoast." Dani shook her head. "I don't know why she didn't."

"Probably saving it for some future weapon," Mark suggested. "Anyway, let's get back to your opinion of me. You were at the point of admitting that I'm not a cad after all."

For the first time in days, Dani felt warm and cheerful. Mark could be pleasant, and as she watched him from the corner of her eye, she thought he even looked a little rugged and outdoorsy with his unshaven face. Maybe he could help her forget her feelings for Josh. Maybe she could learn to appreciate him for himself, instead of comparing him with the ranger who had captured her heart.

She focused her attention on the rushing Merced River spilling over giant boulders, so green with its reflection of the surrounding forest. It reminded her of life—life, full and free-flowing. That's what she wanted. No more tears. No more grieving over the past.

The black car zoomed past tourists standing at the side of the road and in meadows, where they gazed upward at the giant monoliths that surrounded the valley. Dani pointed out the turnoff to the Government Residential Area.

"I have to stop at the Talbotts' for my things." She sighed and rested her head on the seat. "Funny, I didn't think I'd be leaving this way."

Mark steered the car past the government housing and stopped when Dani said, "This is it. I'll only be a minute."

He switched off the ignition and opened his door. "I'll go in with you."

"No, I don't think that's a good idea."

"I think it's a great idea," he said, his words quick and final. "While you get your clothes and belongings together, I'll browse through the house. I still think this 'Lone Ranger' is hiding something."

"Mark, you know everything there is to know about him. Please leave well enough alone!" He was beginning to annoy her again. How could a man be so thoughtful and sensitive one minute and so cold and demanding the next?

"Don't worry your pretty little head. I'm not going to pursue the investigation or the book. I'm a curious guy."

As Dani unlocked the front door, a sense of loss washed over her. She didn't see Edna's smiling face looking up from her crocheting or smell the tantalizing aroma of Martha's pot roast and delicately browned potatoes. And Josh's coat didn't hang over the back of the chair. His voice didn't drift down the stairway in a clear baritone. The house was empty—as empty as Dani's spirit.

"My room's in the back," she said over her shoulder to Mark, who held a cloisonne vase in his hands. "Just stay in here. It won't take long."

"You were right about expensive tastes, Dani. This piece is priceless. Looks like it belongs in a museum." Mark set the vase back on its shelf and started toward the stairs.

"Mark, please. Don't go up there. Give the man some privacy."

"Just get your things, okay? We don't want to be here when the chief and his future squaw arrive!"

The thought of Joshua Talbott and Amanda Jennings walking through the door to discover Dani and Mark in the house sent a spurt of energy through her; she turned from the living room and trotted down the hall to her room. If she worked fast, Mark couldn't spend much time in Josh's room, and they would be away from here and on their way to the Ahwanhee before Josh returned.

She paused a minute to look into Edna's room. Was it only last night that Edna had staggered into the kitchen with a heart attack? Had she heard her conversation with Amanda? Did she believe the only interest Dani had in the Talbotts was as a spy? Dani closed her eyes tightly and felt warm tears prickle her eyelids, squeeze through, and run down her cheeks. She truly loved Edna. What a brave, cheerful spirit the woman had shown! And what faith she had not only in her Lord, but also in her son. How she must have grieved that Josh would bring such a woman as Amanda into his house.

The events of the past months kaleidoscoped through Dani's mind as she tried to piece together the changes in her own heart. The Lord was so real to Edna, and Dani had begun to see his presence working in her own life, yet . . . God seemed remote today. Why would he allow someone as sweet and devoted as Edna to suffer? And why would a man Dani could love and respect be taken from her by a self-indulgent woman like Amanda?

Dani crossed the room and picked up Edna's Bible. The leather cover was soft and faded; Dani held it to her cheek. She felt warmed somehow; all these contrary events would fit into his perfect plan. She didn't need to understand the whys and wherefores. What she did need to do was get out of here!

She set the Bible back on the table and raced to her room to pack. It only took about fifteen minutes to empty the closet and drawers and fill her two suitcases, then she sped back down the hall to call Mark. "Hey, I need your brawn to help me carry these bags to the car."

No answer. Was he still in Josh's room? The thought of his searching through the ranger's private domain caused the blood to pound at her temples. She stormed up the steps, taking two at a time. "Mark, come on. Let's get out of here."

A movement in the corner caught her eye. Mark Hutchinson was stretched out on Josh's waterbed. He leaned on one elbow. "Feel like a little nap?"

"I feel like some fresh air," she said, whirling around and running down the stairs. She had dragged her suitcases through the living room and to the front door when he appeared, smoothing his hair.

"I'll take those," he said. "I get the strong impression that you want to get out of here." A smile played across his lips. "Would you be in such a hurry if the good ranger invited you to his room?"

"I won't lower myself to answer that, Mark." She opened the back of her small car and waited while he placed the bags side by side, then slid into the front seat. "I'll meet you at the Ahwahnee," she said, pulling away from the house in a cloud of dust.

Later, after they had parked their cars and approached the hotel, Dani exclaimed in pleasure, "It's wonderful!"

Mark smiled at her. "You amaze me. I think everything thrills you."

"Well, just look for yourself. Would you expect a massive building like this to be nestled here among the trees?"

The rustic brown hotel seemed to be held up with great pillars of boulders which extended into tall chimneys. In a way, it blended with its surroundings, yet Dani thought it stood apart, majestic and awesome.

Without answering, Mark steered her down the long wooden porch and into the immense lobby with its tiled floors and walls decorated with Indian artifacts.

"My friend here has no reservation," he said to the clerk, "but I'll gladly pay extra for a room."

"Sorry, sir, there aren't any available. August is always filled."

"But I was able to get one with just a phone call," Mark argued.

"We had a cancellation yesterday. You were just lucky."

Dani's face fell along with her hopes. "Guess I'll have to try the lodge."

The clerk interrupted, "Sorry, Miss. They're full up, too."

Mark thanked the clerk, and led Dani to a couch warmed by the sun streaming through the windows. He tipped her chin with a forefinger. "Don't worry, we'll think of something."

Suddenly he snapped his fingers, and his face brightened. "I don't know what you'll think of this idea, but it's the best I can come up with right now. I have a suite of rooms."

"No Mark. We've been through this before."

He held up a hand. "Hear me out. I'm not up to any hanky-panky. I well remember your stand for virtue." He touched his cheek and grimaced in pain. "But as you know, I'll be leaving in the morning anyway, and you could stay in my rooms until you know for sure what's going on with Mrs. Talbott."

Dani's lips formed a thin line. "I can't stay with you. It just wouldn't look right."

Mark shrugged his shoulders and twisted his head from left to right. "Who's looking?"

She watched him closely. He seemed open and

honest; surely he wouldn't take advantage of the situation. Besides, she could lock the door. "Well . . ." she said, hesitating.

"Then it's settled. You come to my rooms, and we'll get freshened up and have dinner here in the restaurant. If you're uncomfortable about going back early, we could take a drive or sit around the lobby all evening."

What other choice did she have? Josh had asked her to leave his home; the lodge was full; there were no other rooms in the hotel. Suddenly she felt very much alone.

"Okay. Since you're going home in the morning," she said tentatively, "and I have your promise to keep our relationship platonic."

"Did I say that?" he teased.

"You inferred it. Now say it," she demanded, her hands on her hips.

Mark smiled and rubbed his stubbly chin. "Platonic, that's us."

Settled in the room, Dani thumbed through park tourist brochures while Mark showered and shaved, and wished her discomfort would pass. Why did she feel guilty when all was so innocent? God knew her heart and motives, and she had nothing to hide.

"Your turn," Mark singsonged, breezing into the room, buttoning his shirt. The whiskers were gone, and once again the suave Mark Hutchinson was on stage, except for his hair. Not yet combed, a strand draped over his eyebrow in a rakish way, and somehow it pleased Dani to see him not quite put together.

She took her time showering and dressing, and was glad for the comfortable suite of rooms where she could recover her poise before facing Edna and Joshua again. She chose a pink cotton dress with a ruffled collar and shocking pink sash. Bright pink enamel earrings and matching pink sandals completed her outfit, and she was pleased with the almost childlike look. No one, especially Mark, could accuse her of impropriety.

Mark in a custom-made navy blue suit and Dani in pink ruffles drew the gazes of other hotel patrons as they entered the expansive dining room. High, beamed ceilings, window-lined walls, and linen-draped tables brought an elegance of city life to the mountains. Men were required to wear ties, and most of the women wore skirts rather than slacks. Although still dusk outside, candles had been lit on each table, blending the rosy glow of fire with the setting sun.

"Oh, Mark, look!" Dani pointed at the long table that stretched almost from one end of the room to the other. Hors d'oeuvres, salads, delicacies of every kind loaded down both sides of the table, but as impressive as that was, her eyes were on the center-piece. A four foot tall ice carving of a trout leaped from the center, its cold blue sheen dripping slowly from pointed fins.

"Did you ever see such a sight?"

"No, I haven't." Mark's eyes were on her. "Beautiful!"

A hostess ushered them to a table next to the window where they had a perfect view of the forest and the towering cliffs beyond. Dani gazed at the panorama, soaking in the beauty she had come to love.

"Would you like me to order for you?" Mark asked as she continued to stare. She hadn't even picked up her menu, and seemed oblivious to her dinner companion.

"Oh, that'll be fine," she answered, her eyes still scanning the view. When she finally pulled her attention away from the now darkening scene, she noticed Mark was nodding to a waiter who poured wine into his glass, then began to fill hers. "Oh, no thank you." Dani held up her hand. "I'll just have water, please."

"As you wish." The waiter nestled the thin green bottle back into a silver tub of ice and walked away.

"Won't you have a glass of wine?"

"You know I don't drink, Mark."

"A glass of wine does not constitute drinking."

"It does to me," she said, lifting her chin. "Maybe it's my strong Christian upbringing—whatever—I don't want it, and I don't need it."

"Okay, okay," Mark said, rubbing his cheek as if he'd been slapped. "I love a woman who knows her own mind. Anyway," he said, tipping his glass toward her before sipping its contents, "here's to you and whatever it is you want out of life."

Dani smiled as she lifted her glass of water to her lips, then put it down. "Thanks, Mark, for being such an understanding employer, and friend. You've opened up my world in many ways."

"How's that?" he asked, draining his glass and reaching for the tall green bottle.

"Well, I've seen a side of life that was foreign to me—Pierre's, that fancy car of yours. I guess some would call it 'Life in the fast lane.'"

"There's a lot more to my life than those things, Dani. Much more." He smiled and reached for her hand. "I might even be competition for that ranger of yours."

"Mark." She drew her hand away. "You promised."

"You're right," he said, pushing back his chair. "Why don't we sample that buffet before they bring our dinner?"

By the time Dani had finished the plate of cold cuts, fruits, and salads, she was almost too full to enjoy her trout.

Mark insisted they were in no hurry. "After all," he said, "where can we go but to our room?"

"We could go for a walk," she said, quickly turning her attention to her plate.

After a long, leisurely meal they walked through the lobby and out into the evening.

Dani smiled up at him. "Thanks for everything. For a few minutes this morning I felt awfully alone and confused. I still don't know what to do after I leave here."

"You're coming back to San Francisco, of course."

"Do you think that's wise? All the staff knows about this assignment. I'd be embarrassed to face them."

Mark stopped and turned toward her. "They don't need to know a thing except the story didn't work out. It won't be the first time I've had a false lead."

"But this wasn't a false one." A frown creased her brow. "And how about Ken Bridges? He seems to be everywhere and know everything. Why did he call Amanda Jennings? We've got to find out what he's up to."

"Don't worry your pretty little head about it. I plan to check into the whole situation when I get back. For now, let's put business behind us and enjoy the present moment."

Mark's words surprised her. In the past, all he wanted to talk about was business, and now he seemed so thoughtful. Kind of pensive somehow. She found the change pleasant but disturbing. After stopping several times to shake pebbles from her shoes, she suggested they return to the hotel.

"But it's only ten o'clock," Mark said, holding his watch so he could read it by moonlight. "What'll we do when we get to the room?"

"I'll go into the bedroom and lock the door, and

you will fix up a bed on the couch." She tipped her head at him, her smile emphasizing the dimple.

They said little as they walked back to the hotel and Dani's mind whirled with ideas for her future. If she didn't return to San Francisco, where would she go? Should she try to find a position in another publishing company?

Mark seemed to read her thoughts. "Dani, I've been thinking, why don't you take a leave of absence, say a couple of weeks, even a month if you need it, and when you decide to come back, your job will be waiting for you."

"Do you mean it?" She was pleased with the offer, and it showed on her face. "Well, that's mighty decent of you, sir," she said slipping her arm around his waist and squeezing. "Thanks."

As soon as they entered the hotel room, Mark switched on the TV, then hung his coat in the closet, loosened his tie, and dropped down onto the low couch. "Want to watch TV a while?" he asked, bending to untie his shoes.

"I think I'll turn in now. It's been a full day, and I didn't sleep much last night." She turned toward the bedroom. "I'll get some blankets for you."

She was closing the closet door when she heard someone beside her. "Dani . . ." Mark's voice was right at her ear, and he touched her shoulder. "I thoroughly enjoyed this evening."

"So did I. In fact, you helped me get over my feeling that I had failed at my job."

"You helped me, too." His voice was soft. "I've never met anyone like you. You're so, well, genuine, and I don't know if you'll like the connotation of innocent. I like that. In fact, I can't believe I'm going to say this, but I might just be in love with you!"

Dani's eyes widened and her mouth dropped open. "You what?"

"Don't be so surprised." He grinned sheepishly. "I know I have a reputation as a man about town, but I've always hoped I would find a woman like you."

"Mark, I . . ."

He touched her lips with his fingers. "Please don't say anything. I know you don't think of me any way other than as an employer, but Dani . . ." Without another word, his arms were around her, and his lips met hers—warm, soft, moist. He held her closer. His kisses swept over her chin, down her neck, and back to her lips again.

With rubbery legs and butterflies in her stomach, Dani pushed against him with both hands. "Don't, Mark. Don't do this."

"But you want me as much as I want you. I know it. I've seen and felt it all evening," he said, still holding her close.

"I'm afraid you misunderstood. I don't feel that way about you," she said, trying to hold back a tide of fear. "If you think you love me, you'll let me go. You won't force me against my will. Please."

"We're adults, Dani. Why are you so afraid to love? You said yourself that you've learned new things from me. Let me teach you how to love."

Dani's voice was firm but gentle. "Not this way, Mark. I don't love you, and even if I did, I told you before—I'm a Christian, and my love will be for my husband—on our wedding night." She pulled away from him as he loosened his hold. "I do respect you though, please don't take that away from me."

Mark stepped back, his face flushed and his breathing heavy. He swept his fingers over his hair and grinned. "Well, at least this time you didn't slap me."

He walked to the bathroom and turned on the light. "I'll brush my teeth and get out of your way for the rest of the night."

"Promise?"

"Promise."

When Dani awoke the next morning, the sun was peeking around the edges of the blinds. She could hear the soft voices of the TV coming from the living room, and was glad Mark was awake. A quick shower and into jeans and sweater, then she opened the bedroom door. The sitting room was empty. On the coffee table was a note. She picked it up and sat down on the couch, where the blankets and pillow still lay unused, to read it.

Dear Dani,

Now it's my turn to walk out on you. I couldn't stay so near you feeling the way I do. I meant every word I said, and if after getting your life in order you can find room for me, I'll be waiting for your call. I do hope you decide to come back to the city. After touching you, kissing you, life will be empty without you.

Love always,
Mark

She dabbed at a tear and reread the note. Why was life so complicated? Even after Mark's confession of love and his passionate kisses, she could only remember that tender moment with Josh by the lake. She knew in her heart that she and Josh were meant for each other, but he was going to marry a woman he didn't love and who didn't love him. There was no point trying to figure out the outcome; right now she only wanted to have some breakfast and get back to Mariposa. How she prayed the news would be good.

The cheerful chatter of guests over coffee, the aroma of bacon and eggs, and the warm sun streaming through the windows only touched the fringes of Dani's mind as she ate her breakfast. Everything tasted the same—dull and flat. Even the scene outside the window held no interest for her, and in a way she was glad. It would be easier to leave the valley while its charms held no sway over her frozen heart.

Her own reflection looked back at her through the window, and as she looked, she could imagine the chief ranger's face beside hers. Her thoughts of him were so powerful, she could smell the spicy clean fragrance that surrounded him.

"Dani, did you hear me?"

She gasped and stared closer at the reflection, then whirled, almost tipping over her coffee cup.

"You must have had quite a night," Josh said, sliding into the chair opposite her.

CHAPTER 9

Josh's words brought a flush of pink to her cheeks. "What do you mean by that?" she flared.

"Do you need to ask?"

Now she was angry. He had jumped to conclusions about her and Mark, and had now come to sit in judgment. Who did he think he was, anyway?

"I wasn't aware that I had to answer to you for my actions. As I remember, I'm no longer in your employ."

"Is that all I've been to you . . . an employer?"

Dani's heart turned over in her chest, and she felt a lump form in her throat. She swallowed hard and twisted the half-filled cup of coffee around in its saucer. "Isn't that the way you wanted it? You've always been quite clear about my duties and responsibilities in your home." Her voice raised as a flood of words broke through the dam of restraint. "And I've done all and more than I was hired to do. I cared for Edna day and night, helping her bathe and dress. We walked and talked for hours. I encouraged her to eat the right foods, and measured out her medication. I cleaned house and cooked when Martha couldn't come. . . ." She took a deep breath. "And, regardless of what you think, I love Edna like my own mother."

The tears streamed down her face, and she dabbed at them with the large yellow napkin. "I admit I've made some giant errors in judgment—going into your room, snooping in your closet—and the biggest one of all was that incident at Mirror Lake."

Josh winced at her last words, but she ignored his expression and stood to leave. "I'm through making wrong moves. Your 'Incomparable Valley' cast a brief spell over me, but now it's broken. I'm going back to San Francisco."

Josh stood, as if he would protest, but Dani turned suddenly and over her shoulder added, "I'll keep in touch with the hospital. I won't forget Edna . . . ever!"

She thought his face was ruddier than usual, and his eyes shone with a misty glow as if he were deeply touched by her words, but she had made her decision. She would leave Yosemite today. No turning back.

After collecting her suitcase and returning the room key, she walked briskly down the long porch and climbed into her car. The sooner she left the valley, the better. Mark would be surprised to hear she had returned to her own apartment so soon. Would it be best to start work right away, or should she do as he suggested and take a couple of weeks off? She did need to change gears, and to go immediately back to the city and Westcoast Publishing Company might strip them.

"Dani! Dani Fuller!"

Through her rearview mirror, she saw Betty McCall waving from the side of the road. She backed up and poked her head out of the window. Betty's wholesome, round face beamed with joy. Slightly plump but attractive, Betty was the picture of a contented wife. She'd been foolish to suspect her and Josh of anything more than friendship.

"Hi!" Dani called. "What's up?"

"I just wondered if you've had any news of Edna." She shrugged her shoulders in a puzzled gesture. "I stopped by the house this morning, but Josh wasn't there and Martha said you'd moved out!"

Before Dani could gather her thoughts, Betty opened the door and slid into the passenger's seat. "Mind if I hitch a ride home? I was out for a morning walk and suddenly feel pooped out."

Dani smiled. Although she didn't know Betty very well, she liked her. She had always been thoughtful about visiting Edna and usually had some cheerful news to share, along with delicious, cholesterol-free cookies. She seemed especially happy this morning.

"Sure, I'll take you home. And on the way, I'll try to answer a few of your questions." She paused as she turned up the road to the rangers' homes. She hoped she wouldn't see Amanda. "As for Edna, I don't know how she is this morning. I'm on my way to the hospital now, then back to San Francisco."

"You mean you're really leaving Yosemite? For good?"

"Well, I'm not needed here anymore. Edna's receiving good care now and will probably be in a convalescent home after her hospitalization. Of course, you know Josh and Amanda are going to be married."

"He's a fool if he marries that phony!"

Dani turned in surprise. Betty's cheery and loving attitude had become bitter. She glanced at Dani and her voice was husky. "We love that guy! He's like a brother to both Bill and me. He's good—too good for her—she'll make his life, and Edna's, miserable."

Dani pulled up in front of Betty's house and turned

off the motor. "Maybe he loves her." She lifted her eyebrows. "Maybe she's not so selfish and willful as she seems."

"Oh, Dani, you don't believe that. You've seen how she manipulates him. All because of something that happened years ago. Something he's suffered enough for."

"Yes, I know about it," Dani said softly.

Betty touched Dani's arm, then tugged gently. "Please come in and have some tea with me before you go. I've wanted to get to know you better, but you've been so busy with Edna, and . . ." She smiled, patting her stomach. "I've been having a little morning sickness."

"You're pregnant?"

Betty nodded, her round cheeks glowing with happiness. "Yes, we found out for sure yesterday. Bill and I have been married for seven years and had about given up. But the Lord is so good. He knows just the right time." She formed a steeple with her fingers, and turned her eyes upward.

Dani felt charmed by the vivacious young woman, and opened the car door to follow her into the house. As she glanced across the roadway to the Talbotts' home, she noticed a movement in the window and thought she recognized Amanda.

Betty bustled around her small, bright kitchen, filling a yellow porcelain teakettle, and putting out flowery china cups. A hand-embroidered cloth draped over the round table, and Dani marvelled at the touches of love through the room. Her eyes flitted from the cloth to a cross-stitched picture on the wall with the words, "Christ is the head of this home." A Bible with well-worn pages marked in red lay open on the table. It reminded her of her mother's Bible.

"You're a Christian, aren't you?" Betty asked, as she poured tea.

"Ah, yes," she stammered, "but not a very good one."

"Oh, we all go through times like that, but we don't have to stay that way." Betty sipped at her tea, then over her cup asked, "You're in love with Josh, aren't you?"

"You don't beat around the bush, do you?"

"There's not time," she said with conviction. "Josh recently rededicated his life to Christ. Then Amanda arrives and threatens to kill herself. We were so happy for him before, but now he has some crazy notion that God wants him to marry Amanda to save her from destroying herself. Personally . . ." Betty pressed her lips together, then hissed, "I think he should call her bluff!"

"You don't believe she'd carry it through?"

"Are you kidding? That gal's too busy squeezing all she can out of life to consider ending it."

Dani nodded. Betty had summed up her opinion of Amanda precisely. Why didn't Josh see through her charade?

Betty continued, "As I see it, men, especially honest, true-blue men, like Josh and my Bill, these kind of men are so trustworthy they think everyone else is. Especially women. They class all females in the 'Mom-apple-pie' category."

Remembering Josh's look that morning in the hotel restaurant, Dani said, "I think you might be wrong about Josh. I don't think he trusts me."

"He just doesn't trust his own feelings about you. You should hear the way he talks to us about you." She smiled. "Why, the lug is in love with you. He just doesn't know it yet."

Dani couldn't believe her ears. Why would Betty say such a thing? She felt her face warm under Betty's gaze, and put her hands to her cheeks.

"You *are* in love with him, aren't you?"

Suddenly, the sound of a car skidding on gravel, hurried steps up the sidewalk, and the opening of the front door caught their attention. Joshua Talbott stormed into the room, his eyes wide, and his face grim.

"That crazy woman!" he shouted, waving a piece of note paper. "Now she's on her way to the hospital to tell Mother Dani isn't a nurse, and something about her being a spy! Can you believe that?" He looked wildly from Betty to Dani. "She's crazy. She knows any startling news will kill Mother."

Betty was out of her chair and reached up to put her hands on Josh's shoulders. "Listen here, you big ape. Edna would never believe such a wild story. She wasn't born yesterday, you know. But Amanda's presence could really upset her." She paused, then snapped her fingers. "Tell you what—if you went after her, she'd be even more determined, and no telling what she'd do—so you stay here *with Dani.*" She emphasized the last two words. "And I'll drive down to headquarters, pick up Bill, and we'll head her off. How long ago did she leave?"

"I passed her coming up the hill only a few minutes ago."

"Okay, see you soon. Don't worry, we'll bring her back. And Dani, you don't need to answer my question. The answer is written all over your face." Betty was out the door and into her car before either of them could protest.

Josh smiled weakly and shook his head, the tension leaving his face. "She's quite a whirlwind, isn't she?" He raked his fingers through his hair. "If anyone can persuade Amanda to give up her plan, she can." A slight chuckle shook his shoulders. "I think Betty McCall could charm the stripe off a skunk."

"I think you're right," Dani said softly, aware that she was alone with the man she had determined to

132

forget. She didn't trust her bruised emotions, and wanted to get away as soon as possible. "I wish I'd gotten to know her better."

"You could if you stayed longer."

"We've already discussed this."

"You discussed it. I didn't get to say a word."

"My work is finished here. I need to get on with my life." Her voice had a cold, hard ring, and Josh studied her several moments before speaking.

"I don't understand you at all. You're the most unpredictable woman I've ever met."

"And you, Joshua Talbott, chief ranger, are a dope!" Dani turned and stalked through the house and down the walk with Josh following close behind.

"What do you mean by that?"

"Never mind. Betty was right about you. She said you're so trustworthy, you think everyone else is, though I can't say you've ever shown much trust in me. Anyway, you ought to take another close look at your fiancée. You just admitted that she's crazy."

As Dani bent to get into her car, Josh grabbed her arm, pressing his fingers into the soft flesh until she winced. "Let go of me!"

"No, I'm not letting you leave here until I have a word with you. Come with me."

Still gripping her arm, he pulled her up a narrow path which passed behind the McCalls' home. Dani's breath came in spurts as she attempted to keep up with him. Every time she slowed down, his fingers tightened, so she decided not to resist. Finally, they reached the summit, and he released her arm, then stepped to the edge of a cliff overlooking the valley. Dani watched from a distance and rubbed the tender spot on her arm. What was he going to do now?

After long, silent moments, he turned toward her, glancing tenderly at her arm. "I'm sorry, I don't want to hurt you . . . ever." He held out a hand. "Come here, Dani."

133

She stepped back and widened her eyes in alarm. "You don't plan to push me over, do you?"

"Please?" The warm brown eyes pleaded, and the mannish dimples beckoned. In spite of all her declarations, she was drawn to him and thrilled as he slipped his arm around her shoulders.

Pounding heart and racing pulse. Secure and warm. She looked up at his profile. A light breeze played in his hair, pulling auburn waves down over the broad forehead. His nose flared slightly as he inhaled deeply of the warm mountain air, and the thick mustache swept lightly over his upper lip. Her eyes dropped to the brown ringlets that peeked over his shirt collar. She had never felt the powers of her own femininity stirred so deeply, or been so aware of the touch of a masculine presence. For a moment she felt giddy and leaned against him for support. His arm tightened around her and his heart beat fiercely against her shoulder.

"Have you ever seen anything more magnificent?" His eyes scanned the vista before them, and his voice had a prayerlike tone. "Climb the mountains and get their good tidings. Nature's peace will flow into you as sunshine flows into trees." He smiled down at her. "John Muir may have stood in this place when he wrote that, but I think I would have called it God's peace." His lips brushed her hair and he said softly, "Dani, I can't let you go."

With a steadiness in her voice that surprised her, she asked, "You mean you've decided *not* to marry Amanda?" She pulled away from him and looked up into his eyes.

"I have to marry her . . . I'm responsible for her illness, whether it's physical or mental."

"That's no basis for marriage, Josh, and you know it." Dani stepped back, fighting against her desire to touch him. "It's either Amanda or me—you can't have both of us. If you're going to marry **Amanda**, then do it. Just leave me alone. I have to get on with my life. I don't see how you can talk about God in one breath, then play with my affections in the next."

"I know . . . I'm so confused . . ."

"Well, you can just be confused without me. I'm returning to San Francisco. At least Mark Hutchinson is interested in only one woman at a time, and at the moment it happens to be me."

Why did she say that? It sounded so childish and totally opposite from the way she felt. Josh's face reddened and he narrowed his eyes, then shoved his hands into his pockets.

"You're right, you should go back to your city boyfriend. There's no point in your staying here!"

As Dani drove past the entrance station and out of the park, the clock on the Honda dashboard read 1:30. She wouldn't be able to reach San Francisco at a decent hour without pushing herself, and although an overnight stop at Lodi was feasible, she didn't want to face her parents yet. They were too observant and would ask questions she was unable to answer honestly. Perhaps in a few days, she would be ready for a short visit, but for tonight, she would stay in Mariposa.

Passing the cheap motel where she had stayed her first time through, she drove until she found one listed in her AAA Tour Guide. It was clean and modern, and she may as well be comfortable, especially if she decided to remain a few days to be near Edna. She deposited her bags in the room, swept a brush through her hair, and pointed her car toward the hospital. She had been so wrapped up in her own problems, she had hardly given Edna a thought. Would she be improved today? Had the McCalls apprehended Amanda in time?

With a sense of dread, she entered the hospital and headed for the intensive care unit.

"May I help you?" asked a crisply uniformed young woman.

"I've come to see Edna Talbott."

"Oh, she's gone. I guess you didn't hear."

A cold wave of fear washed over Dani while her knees turned to water and the blood rushed from her face. "She's . . ."

"Oh, no, she's alive, and much better today," the nurse consoled as she guided her to a chair and patted her shoulder.

"But I don't understand." Dani's face was pale and drawn as she lifted it to the nurse.

"She was transferred to Merced by ambulance this morning. They have better facilities for her there. Then as she gains more strength, probably in a day or two, the doctors plan to move her to Sacramento."

Dani's head swam in confusion. "Why must she be moved around so much? If she's better, why can't she go home?" She twisted her hands in her lap and stared intently at the young woman.

"She's going to need surgery."

"Oh, how awful!"

The nurse's voice was reassuring. "No, it's really a very good sign. Mrs. Talbott is basically a strong woman. She's not a smoker, not overweight, and she has a positive attitude. All these things make her an excellent candidate for open-heart surgery."

"Open-heart?"

"Yes, the doctor suspects a leaking valve needs replacement, and he also thinks a by-pass will give her many more years."

Dani breathed deeply, afraid to ask the next question, but knowing she must. "Could something she saw or heard have caused this last attack?"

"Well, I think I could safely say that it was

inevitable. According to the doctor, the first one caused more damage than was discovered in earlier tests ''

Dani sighed with relief. "Then I guess there's nothing I can do . . . but pray."

The nurse smiled indulgently. "Well, the Shumway heart team in Sacramento is one of the best in the country. She'll be fine."

"Does her son know about this?" Dani was certain he didn't, or he wouldn't have been so concerned about Amanda's note.

"We've tried to reach him, but he wasn't home all night, and we haven't been able to contact him today. We did leave word at Park Headquarters, though."

After Dani assured the nurse that she was feeling better, she left the hospital, suddenly conscious of a gnawing pain in the pit of her stomach. She drove down the main street until she found an attractive café and went inside. Not wanting to face incoming customers, she chose a booth in the corner and slid in, her back to the door. After ordering, she pulled a spiral notebook from her purse, and began to write in her daily journal.

Assignment completed. A failure, but complete. I guess I'd call it a complete failure! I will say, I'm a different person today than when I first arrived at Yosemite. When I started this assignment, I thought I knew everything; now I'm sure I know nothing. I don't feel as carefree as I did a couple of months ago. I'm sure I've done some growing up, and I know what it feels like to have loved and lost. Not good!

Dani paused in her writing to sink her teeth into what must be the most delicious hamburger she had ever tasted, then she wiped her mouth and began to write again.

Maybe Josh is right. If Amanda is really ill as he believes, his strength and faith in Christ could be the miracle cure she needs. But if she's really as vindictive as . . .

"Talbott will go for it."

"You don't know Joshua like I do."

Several booths behind her, someone was discussing Josh. Carefully, slowly, she turned her head to see who it was, then gasped in surprise. Ken Bridges and Amanda Jennings sat on the same side of the booth, their backs to her, bending over the table. What were they up to? Dani perked up her ears and sat upright, straining to catch their conversation.

"With the old lady and that Fuller dame out of the way, what's to stop you?" The gutteral voice sent a shiver up her spine.

"Why are you so interested, Mr. Bridges? Surely the money I've promised you isn't your only motive in reducing him to an office boy." The whine sickened Dani.

"I have plans that don't concern you."

"Anything to do with Joshua Talbott concerns me."

"Anything involving his money, you mean." Bridges' words were a snarl. "I have something much more profitable in mind than a paltry inheritance."

Then as their voices dropped, Dani could sense movement while they gathered papers together, latched them in a case, and walked out of the café. She wondered if Ken Bridges had left the check on the table.

CHAPTER 10

DANI COULD HARDLY BELIEVE the sense of weariness that had come over her. No wonder—the happenings of the past few days would bring stress to the most strong-hearted. First, Amanda's arrival, then the scene with her, and Edna's heart attack. Dani's hand instinctively went to her chest as she remembered that night. And could she ever forget Josh's accusing look when Amanda broke the news of the falsified resume? But that didn't compare with the searching accusation of this morning—he presumed she had spent the night with Mark Hutchinson. Yet she couldn't deny it, could she? She was in his room; who would believe her innocence?

And now, Amanda and Ken Bridges were plotting together. How had they met? Although she could understand Amanda's motives to cash in on Marlena's inheritance, what was Ken up to?

Dani tossed and turned on the motel bed, trying to forget the events of the day. It was over and done with, and she was on her way home. Tomorrow she would drive directly to her apartment in San Francisco without stopping in Lodi. After that? Only God had the answer.

When Dani awoke, she felt confused. She could see through the window that the sun had set and the sky was a pale gray. Her narrow gold watch showed that it was seven-thirty—time for dinner. After splashing her face with cold water, she combed through her hair, and clipped it to the top of her head in a ponytail. A lightweight blue flannel shirt would feel good in the cool evening air, and jeans and her favorite jogging shoes were perfect for a nice long walk to the café.

Amanda would be safely back in Josh's home by now, and Ken on his way to Westcoast Publishing Company, or whatever rock it was he lived under.

The sultry August afternoon had been blown away by a cool breeze that swept down from the High Sierra, and Dani inhaled deeply of the crisp mountain air. How she dreaded her return to the traffic and smog of the city.

As she remembered, the café where she had lunch was about a mile from the motel, and not feeling at all apprehensive in the small town, she strolled aimlessly down one narrow street after another, stopping to admire old frame houses and peering with interest into shops filled with antiques and early vintage junk. She seemed to be leaving the business district and with a quickening pulse, realized she had taken a wrong turn.

The sky was darker now—a bluish gray that reminded her of a watercolor painting in her apartment—and she lifted her head wondering if it would rain earlier than usual this year. That's when she heard a footstep behind her. And another. As she turned to see who it was, a hand reached out and grabbed her shoulder.

"Well, this *is* my lucky night. It's Goody-Two-

Shoes!" Dani could smell the alcohol on his breath, and see a strange wild look in his eyes.

She pulled away and began to run.

Down the rutted road and around the corner. The fat man wouldn't be able to catch her. She shuddered to think Ken Bridges had been following her. She stopped to lean against an old building, its paint cracked and peeling. Her breath came in spurts, labored and painful. Running in a high altitude was nothing like her runs through Golden Gate Park.

She tried to orient herself. She must get back to her motel. She couldn't see any glow in the sky from the short main street where neon signs lit the store fronts. She must pull herself together. After all, she was a city girl, and had been on her own for several years. She had good sense and a clear mind. Then why did she feel so confused and afraid?

"Oh, Lord, please show me where to go," she said aloud.

Sometimes jogging, sometimes running, always straining her eyes for a familiar landmark, Dani fought back panic. Several blocks away, she caught sight of a flashing red sign and sighed in relief. She turned the corner.

"So here you are." Ken's words slurred together, and his viselike grip held her arms down. "We'll have to stop meeting like this."

"Let go of me, or I'll scream," Dani warned.

Ignoring her threats, Ken twisted her around, holding her back against his body, and covering her mouth with his hand. "I think I'll have the last word this time, Miss Fuller."

If only she had been facing him, she could stomp on his instep, but she was helpless. His strength amazed and frightened her. What was he going to do? And could she talk him out of it?

He half pushed, half dragged her into a narrow alley

141

and shoved her against a building. She struggled with all the power she had, but was unable to move. She opened her mouth and tried to bite his hand, but he clamped it so tightly, she couldn't close her teeth.

His face was beside her ear now, and his hot, pungent breath sent a wave of nausea through her. "Now Goody-Two-Shoes, it's my turn," he hissed. "I've watched you sneak off into the woods with Talbott, and into hotels with Hutchinson. Now I want a taste of your favors."

Disgust and revulsion sent a shudder through her body, but she decided if she relaxed and made him believe she liked his suggestion, she might catch him off guard and be able to escape.

"Mm, mm," she mumbled.

"You gonna be a good girl and not scream?" he growled.

She nodded her head up and down, and rolled her eyes at him as he peered into her face.

"No one would hear you, anyway. I waited until you got up here by these deserted buildings." He breathed heavily. "I've wanted you for a long time, since that first day in Hutchinson's office. I thought, now there's a fresh young doll I could really go for."

Dani was afraid she would be sick, but attempted a smile with her eyes. She leaned invitingly against him. *Oh God, help me.*

Ken's swollen and whiskery face brushed against hers. "You gonna behave yourself?"

"Uh-huh, uh-huh," she mumbled, nodding again.

"Okay, but if you make one sound, it'll be your last." He loosened his grip. "You won't get away like you did that other time."

Dani's eyes widened. "Huh?"

"Who did you think was giving you a little nudge down the highway that night? If Talbott hadn't been in the wrong place at the wrong time, I'd have pushed you off the road."

So he was the one. She'd suspected him for a minute, but had dismissed it. In fact, she'd forgotten all about that incident.

"You!" she managed to say through his sweaty fingers. "But why?"

"That's all in the past now, isn't it, doll? We can have ourselves a real good time if you just cooperate. Those young skinny guys can't compare to an older, well-built man like me."

Dani tried for another smile, hoping he could see it in the darkness. He loosened his grip, and as his fingers relaxed, she licked her bruised lips. Her teeth ached, and her jaw felt out of joint, but she cooed, "Ken, I had no idea you were attracted to me. Why didn't you tell me before?"

He turned her around and pulled her close, breathing heavily on her neck. "Couldn't you guess?" He motioned with his head. "Let's go to my car, it's down there."

"Well, that sounds all right, but I do have a comfortable hotel room. Why don't we go there?" She tried to sound seductive while praying in her heart, *Help me, God, help me!*

"Say, you're all right," he said, planting a wet kiss on her cheek. "Not a Goody-Two-Shoes, after all."

As the fat man released his grip to lead her to his car, she bolted.

A great surge of energy filled her veins, and she ran faster and longer than she dreamed possible. Finally, she saw a small white building, its windows orange from the light within. Strains of music drifted out into the evening air. A church! *Oh, thank you, Lord. Thank you!*

Dani glanced over her shoulder before entering. Ken Bridges was nowhere in sight, so she shoved the heavy wooden door open a crack and slipped in. Rows and rows of high-backed pews were filled with

143

people, and it wasn't even Sunday. Wednesday, wasn't it? She kept her head down as she slid into the back pew, knowing she must look a sight. Her hair had fallen around her shoulders, and as she touched her tender lips, she felt dried blood. The top buttons had been ripped off her shirt, and she wrapped her arms about herself, trembling violently.

A woman with gray hair and a kind face unobtrusively leaned toward her, a sweater in her hand. Dani took it gratefully and smiled, shoving her arms into the sleeves and buttoning it to the neck. She felt soiled and invaded. She wanted to go home. Home to Mom and Dad. They loved her . . . always had. To protect their only daughter from worldliness and a wasted life—that had been their reason for holding her so close.

As the preacher's words penetrated her turmoil, she remembered the many times her parents had reminded her that she was God's child, and that he loved her, too!

Sitting in that peaceful room among a group of Christians, Dani knew that she had come home at last. The tears coursed down her face, cleansing and healing her past rebellions and her very present doubts and fears. As she sat there, she was oblivious to the worshipers as they left, speaking softly to one another.

"Is there anything I can do?" The woman who had given her the sweater was beside her, a slight frown on her brow. "I'm Dorothy Fisher, the pastor's wife. I can see you're troubled, and if I, or we, can be of help—"

She didn't finish her sentence because Dani took her hand and squeezed it.

"Yes, you can help me. I'd like to speak to the pastor, and you, too, if I may."

Mrs. Fisher handed her a tissue, then excused herself. "I'll get my husband."

"Oh, that's okay, I'll come to his study," she said, blowing her nose and standing up.

She followed the woman to the front of the church where the pastor had just finished praying with two teenaged girls. He looked up with a smile, then as he saw Dani, concern showed on his face, and he held out a hand. Dani thought it felt like the largest and warmest hand she'd ever taken.

"I'm Pastor Bob," he said. "What can I do for you?" His eyes swept over her. "Have you been in an accident?"

A few minutes later, Dani sat in the study with Dorothy Fisher's arm around her shoulder. She poured out her narrow escape from Ken Bridges, then told them about Josh and Edna Talbott and Mark Hutchinson and her job at Westcoast. Over an hour passed before she finished her story.

"I've been running from God for a long time. I thought I knew what was best for me. But now I know his way is best." She paused, wiping at her eyes. "It's been a long time since I prayed a real prayer. Would you help me? I mean, I want to tell God I'm coming back to him, for good." Her heart felt light and so full of joy, she thought it might burst.

Together, the stocky white-haired man, his wife, and Dani knelt on the wooden floor and talked to God. When they finished, they hugged each other and for the first time in many months, even years, Dani knew that there was a purpose for her life. God would show her what it was. She was his, totally his.

"Dani, I've been thinking," Pastor Bob said with concern in his eyes, "it wouldn't be wise for you to go back to your motel tonight. We'll go with you to get your things, then you come home with us." He smiled as she nodded. "You can stay as long as you like. You've had a scare, and on top of all your other experiences, I think you need a few days of peace and quiet."

145

"That's a marvelous idea, dear." Dorothy patted her husband's arm, then smiled at Dani. "Yes, you come home with us for a few days."

The two days with the Fishers was like a taste of heaven to Dani. The peace and serenity of their lives reflected in their home.

She slept late every morning, then joined them for devotions where Pastor Bob would read a portion of Scripture, and Dorothy gave practical ways to live it out. They invited her to set spiritual goals for herself each day, such as reading a chapter from the Bible, or memorizing a verse she liked. They closed this time together with prayer and singing a hymn. How like her early life. "I didn't tell you before," she said the morning of her departure, "but I was raised in a parsonage."

"Your father's a pastor?" Dorothy beamed. "You know, I had an inkling. Some of the things you said reminded me of our son."

"Yes, Bill is still running away from God," Pastor Bob remarked. "But Dani, your fresh commitment to Christ has given us encouragement. We both," he said, slipping his arm around his wife, "believe God sent you to us at a time when we needed you."

"You needed me?" Dani could hardly believe her ears. "God used me to bless you?" She would always marvel at his timing. It was just as Betty had said. Their baby was according to God's schedule, not theirs.

"And don't you worry, dear," Dorothy said, hugging her, "we'll keep praying for your friends. If it's in God's plan that you and that young ranger get together, no one can stop it!"

After a tearful parting, Dani was on her way to San Francisco. She had said many farewells lately. It shouldn't be too difficult to say them again to the

Westcoast crowd and Mark. He must be wondering where she was. Or had Ken Bridges contacted him? Thinking about Ken and her last encounter with him gave her the shivers, but instead of brooding as in the past, she began to sing, "How great thou art; How great thou art!" The newfound joy and peace seemed to lift her out of her present problems. Why had she tried so hard and so long to get away from God's love?

As Dani crossed the Oakland Bay Bridge, she thought the sun looked like a giant orange balancing on a blue saucer. She was glad the Saturday evening traffic wasn't heavy, and soon she began to spot familiar faces out for walks and chatting on front porches. It felt good, so good, to be back on home territory that she bounded out of her car the minute she had parked and ran up the walk to her apartment building—an old Victorian mansion that had been converted to accommodate six renters. Even the ancient elevator, once used by a wealthy gambler's family, was still in operation. Dani didn't bother with it, though, and ran up the stairs, a suitcase in each hand. She wondered how her plants had fared. Did the girl across the hall water them as she had promised?

The apartment smelled a little musty and a fine layer of dust covered all the tables. Dani threw open the tall windows to let the ocean breezes in, and the closed-up odors disappeared. Her favorite fern had grown large. She spritzed it with her mister and found a cloth to dust the furniture.

Yosemite was far behind her now. Her life in Christ was new from beginning to end. No more crying over Joshua Talbott. No more bitterness for Amanda Jennings. And Mark. She'd see him on Monday morning and tell him about Ken Bridges. He really should have nothing to do with that man.

As a blanket of night covered the city, Dani curled up on her rattan sofa with a cup of instant coffee and opened her old Bible which she had dusted off after she had tackled the furniture. After reading several chapters in the Book of John, she began to make a list of things she must do to get her life in order. "Dear Lord," she said aloud as if she could see his Presence, "please show me what to do. I'm tired of botching up."

On Monday morning, she would notify Mrs. Edgerton that she was moving out; go to Westcoast and clean out her desk, if it weren't already occupied by some new researcher; make an appointment to see Mark and give her notice; call her folks and ask if she could come home until she could decide what to do. She read through her list. If all went well, in a week or two, she would be back in Lodi. It would seem strange, but she knew her parents would be happy to have her. She had been a worry to them for many years.

Leaning her head back and closing her eyes, she saw the image of the sun setting in the ocean. She would love to spend a day at the ocean before leaving the coast. Point Reyes. That's where she would go. Tomorrow, Sunday morning, she would take a trip up to the National Seashore, and just spend the day alone. It would be wonderful.

Tired and happy with her decisions, Dani went to her room and snuggled down into bed, pulling the soft quilt high around her chin. It was good to be home.

With a start, Dani's eyes flew open. A pounding had awakened her. She leaned up on one elbow and listened. No one knew she was back in San Francisco. Who would come over this early, anyway?

She slipped a robe over her shoulders, shoved her hair behind her ears, and padded to the door. For the

148

umpteenth time, she wished for a peephole in her door. "Who is it?"

"It's me. Mark. When did you get back?"

Dani opened the door a crack, and when she saw that it really was Mark, she stepped aside to let him in.

"Last night," she said, wrapping her robe tightly about her. "I planned to come in to the office tomorrow."

"You weren't going to call me before that? I was going to check on your apartment, then I saw your car out front." His eyes swept over her face and rested on her lips. "I've missed you, Dani."

His voice and expression brought back memories of their last evening together. She flushed under his ardent gaze.

"May I stay a while?" he asked, flopping down in a chair. "There's lots for you to tell me."

"There sure is," she said politely, "but as you can see, you woke me up. I'm not prepared for visitors."

"Well, you go ahead and get ready. I'll fix some coffee." He stood up and started toward the kitchen. "I've looked in on your place several times, so I know my way around."

Dani did as she was told, and rushed through her shower, combed her hair into a thick braid, and pulled on her faded Levi's and a red turtleneck sweater. Walking into the kitchen, she announced, "I can't visit long, though. I've plans for the day."

"Oh? Anyone I know?"

"Yep."

"Who?"

"Just me." She sipped the hot coffee from a thick mug and dabbed at a drop that dribbled down the side. "I'm going to Point Reyes, and I don't want to be rude, but I have to get an early start if I want to see everything I've planned."

Mark cocked his head to one side. "You wouldn't want a tagalong, would you?" He held up three fingers, Boy-Scout fashion. "I promise not to get in the way, or hug or kiss you! On my honor."

"Oh, all right, come along then. But you've made promises before. This time I'm going to be alert. We're taking my car, and if you try any funny business I'm dumping you!"

"Ouch," he groaned, grasping his chest. "You really know how to hurt a guy."

Mark did most of the talking as Dani drove across the Golden Gate Bridge and up Highway 1. She concentrated on maneuvering the sharp curves as they wound their way up the rocky coastline. "Want to stop at Stinson?" Mark asked as the road reached the summit before heading back down to sea level.

"No, I have a one-track mind. I plan to spend as much time as possible at Point Reyes."

"Why the sudden interest? Are you into National Parks now?"

She knew by the tone of his voice that he was hinting for some information about Joshua Talbott, and her feelings for him, but she ignored the inference and began to relax as the road became less dangerous. "Mark, I had a run-in with Ken Bridges in Mariposa. He attacked me."

"He what?" Mark's face paled.

"I escaped, but he did give me quite a scare." She glanced toward him. "I also overheard him that same day talking to Amanda Jennings in a café—something about bringing Josh down from a ranger to an office boy. They were talking about money, too."

Mark frowned and rubbed his chin. "I don't understand. I told Bridges to forget the whole project. He said he already had."

"I think he has a project of his own going. Maybe

he's writing his own exposé. He evidently learned about Amanda Jennings and contacted her. They're both determined to hurt Josh," Dani said, her voice cracking. "I can't understand why."

"I'll look into it, Dani, tomorrow. He's up to something, and I'll get him." Mark frowned and said soberly, "If he had hurt you . . ."

"I don't want to see anyone hurt, Mark. Especially Edna." She slowed for a car pulling a boat and faced Mark.

"Believe it or not, I don't want to cause problems for the Talbotts, either. They're okay. I even like the 'Lone Ranger,' in spite of myself."

A little smile dimpled Dani's cheek as she said under her breath, "Quimo sabe!"

She felt relaxed with Mark today. No longer did he intimidate her with his air of superiority. As long as he treated her like a friend, and nothing more, their day together would be pleasant.

After stopping briefly at the Bear Valley Visitor Center for brochures and maps, Dani drove down the road to the little town of Inverness.

"Do you realize," Mark said, looking up from the map, "that we're driving right on top of the San Andreas Fault. One good shake and we'll float away from the mainland on our own little island."

She smiled, then followed his gaze as he pointed out a small building at the side of the road. "There's a French restaurant we can try on the way back tonight."

"You and your French restaurants. No thanks, Mark. I'm alert, remember?"

"We have to eat."

"How about a good old-fashioned hot dog?"

The rest of the day, Mark was quieter than usual. He seemed to sense that she wanted to be alone mentally, if not physically, and trailed behind her like an obedient puppy. They walked down the beach at Drake's Bay, Mark sedate even in sports clothes, and Dani kicked off her shoes, digging her toes into the cool sand with every step. She lifted her face to the fine salty spray and imagined the Indians who met Francis Drake on his arrival so long ago.

They stopped at a lunchroom at the bay for coffee and a hot dog, and watched the sea gulls swoop and sway over them, squawking for bits of bread. Later, curiosity drew them to the point where the lighthouse was situated.

"Three hundred steps down," Mark warned. "Don't forget, what goes down must climb up!"

The view from the point was spectacular, and Dani listened intently as a woman ranger explained that this point of land was one of the most hazardous on the Pacific Coast. "The water around here is a graveyard of ships."

"I'm so glad I came," Dani panted, as they climbed back up the steps. "I can see that I'll have to come back when I have more time, though." As she heard and felt the pounding roar of the waves against the rocks, she was thrilled and began to hum "Rock of Ages, cleft for me."

"Dani," Mark said, tugging at her braid, "you're different today."

"Oh, I guess it's my little-girl hairdo. If I'd known it would be so cold here, I'd have left it down."

"No, I'm not talking about your hair. Anyway, you could let it down now."

"Oh, no," she argued, "it would be a giant bush of kinks."

When they reached the car and stopped to catch their breath, Mark repeated, "What's so different about you? You seem to have a quiet strength I've never seen before."

Dani smiled broadly, her dimple deepening on her

cold, rosy cheek. "I do have a strength I didn't have before, Mark."

They were in the car and speeding up the road before he pursued his question further. From the corner of her eye, she watched him light a cigarette and inhale deeply. "So what is it that makes you so strong? Been drinking your Ovaltine?"

"It's Christ," she answered simply. "I've given my life to Christ."

"Oh." Mark cocked his head. "Edna Talbott rubbed off on you, huh?"

"Well," she said, smiling over at him, "not exactly. As I told you before, I've been a Christian for many years, but I haven't been living for God."

Mark frowned and snubbed out the cigarette. "I don't know what you're talking about, but if it makes you happy, I'm glad for you."

Without hesitation, Dani blurted, "Have you ever given any thought to your eternal destiny?"

He stiffened, and she could see the cords in his neck enlarge. "Two things I never talk about . . . religion and politics."

"That's not true, Mark. All of your books are political," she said with an impish grin.

"You got me there. Well, there's one thing I never talk about . . ." Glancing at the ranger station, he didn't finish his sentence but pointed toward the Visitor Center as they drove past.

A tall auburn-haired ranger leaned against a park truck, and as he turned toward them, Mark exclaimed, "Isn't that Joshua Talbott?"

CHAPTER 11

DANI HAD KNOWN INSTANTLY that the ranger outside the white frame building was not Josh. She knew the shape of his head, the way he pulled at his mustache, his every gesture, yet hearing his name and seeing someone who resembled him created a kaleidoscope of confusion in her heart. She pressed harder on the accelerator and sped up the highway leading back to the city.

"Hey, let me get my seat belt on!" Mark teased. "You really don't want to see that guy again." He leaned forward studying her pale face. "Or do you?"

Dani snapped a look in his direction. "Let's not ruin a perfect day. I've left Yosemite and everyone I met there behind me . . . forever."

Mark leaned back in the small bucket seat and lit a cigarette. "H'm, I'm glad to hear that. Maybe there's room for me in your life, after all."

"Mark, please."

"Now you have to give me an A+. I didn't touch you once all day, and haven't even asked if I had a chance." He sighed an exaggerated groan. "And I avoided mentioning our, ah, night at the Ahwahnee."

"And I appreciate it," she said coldly. "Let's leave it that way."

He rubbed his cheek. "I'm not sure, but I think I've been slapped again."

She smiled, still keeping her eyes on the narrow, winding road. She would be glad to be back at the apartment, because although the day had been pleasant, it wasn't what she had hoped for. She needed a day alone, a day to think, to pray, to discover God's plans for her.

Yet Mark Hutchinson was still her employer, and she wasn't convinced she should give up her job. Besides, she had to admit to herself, she had enjoyed his company. He was charming, and, she glanced over at his angular profile, yes, he was extremely good looking.

Throughout the rest of the trip over the hills, across the bridge, and up the busy streets leading to her home, they were silent. Mark seemed to sense her discomfort, and even looked a little strained himself. When she pulled into the parking lot beside her apartment house, he yanked the keys from the ignition and dropped them into his shirt pocket.

"Before we leave this car, I want to get some things straight," he said, placing a hand on her shoulder. "You have me going around in circles. I've never known a woman like you. One minute you're sophisticated and adult, the next, an innocent child. I can't think straight anymore. I'll be honest, Dani." His gray eyes shone with a warm glow as pink rays of the setting sun slanted into the car window. "I'm not sure if I'm in love . . . or just fascinated."

Dani laughed. "Well, thanks for your honesty. I think your male ego has been a little crumpled, that's all. I like you, Mark, I really do, and I think you like me, but you're not in love with me. We just don't have enough in common for our relationship to grow into anything more than what it is now."

"You don't have a chance with Talbott, you know." His words were icy, and his fingers pressed into her shoulder.

"Who says I want one?" She pulled away and stared back at him. "I'm not interested in an involvement of any kind." She hoped her voice sounded more convincing than she felt. She turned from him and opened the car door, and as Mark came around to meet her, she held out a hand. "I'll take my keys now."

"Let me come in for a while," he said, standing close to her.

"I'm very tired, Mark. If it's okay, I'd still like to take that short leave of absence." She held out her hand again. "Keys?"

His voice was husky as he leaned over her, "Dani, I don't expect you to ever love me, at least with the kind of love you're looking for, but I know I could make you happy." He backed her up against the car. "Let me try."

She stepped aside, but his arms went around her, and he pulled her against him, pressing his lips hard against hers. When she pulled her face aside, he said, "You don't have to marry me. I'm not the marrying kind, anyway, but you could move in with me!"

"What?" She couldn't believe her ears; her jaw dropped open.

"Oh, I know you're an old-fashioned girl, but I think even you have needs!"

"Give me my keys. I'll try to forget you even suggested such an arrangement, especially after I made it quite clear not only how I felt about you, but also about my commitment to Christ." She grabbed at the keys he dangled in front of her and spun around.

157

"I quit. A job doesn't mean that much to me. Neither do you."

Now Mark's eyes were dark with rage. "There's a word for women like you. You tease and flirt, then when you get a man's blood to the boiling point, you pretend to be so holy and pure." His lip turned up in a sneer. "I wouldn't be surprised if you and Talbott were a little 'closer' than you admit!"

Dani's first inclination was to strike that smirking face, but instead she turned and calmly replied, "I won't even respond to such a statement.

Too furious to cry, she walked purposefully into the Victorian house, up the stairs, and into her apartment, all the while praying for a gracious spirit.

The following week, Dani packed and stored most of her belongings, taking only the clothes she would need until she found a new place to live, or at least knew her next step. She looked forward to moving back to the small San Joaquin Valley town where she had spent most of her life.

"Oh, honey, we'll be so glad to have you," her dad had said when she asked if she could come home. "You stay as long as you want. You always have a room here."

It would be strange living at home again after all these years, but she only planned to stay until she had found a job or knew what God's plans were for her. The possibility of returning to school had crossed her mind.

The drive from San Francisco to Lodi was enjoyable. The high fields of corn and acre after acre of grapes were almost ready to harvest. Her parents' home was on a small plot of land west of town, adjacent to the church where her father had served so many years as pastor. Now that he had retired, he ministered primarily to shut-ins and senior citizens, but continued living in the original parsonage. The new pastor, her mother had said, was a young man with a wife and two small children. They had chosen to buy their own home not far from the church.

As Dani drove up to the well-kept white stucco house, her mother and father burst through the front door, their arms open wide, gathering her close and both talking at once. Later, after they had put her things in her old bedroom and she had stretched out in a comfortable chair with her feet on the hassock, her mother asked, "Now what's this good news you've promised us? We can't wait to hear."

"Well," Dani said, smiling over her glass of iced tea, "I have both good news and bad. First the bad, I don't have a job."

"Thank the Lord," her mother exclaimed. "I thought it was something more serious."

"I know you didn't approve of my working in San Francisco, but Mom, this means I don't have any source of income."

"Don't you worry, dear." Mrs. Fuller patted Dani's knee. "You'll find something. You worked for that publishing company for two years. They'll surely give you a good reference."

"And those people up in Yosemite. They'll put in a good word for you, too," her dad added.

Dani smiled, imagining the kind of references both Mark and Josh would give, but she hurried on, "Now for the good news." She set her glass down and folded her hands in her lap. "This is something I know you've wanted to hear for a long time—I've come back to the Lord!"

Tears instantly flooded Mrs. Fuller's eyes and her nose reddened as she reached out and took Dani in her arms. Dani hugged her back, marvelling how soft and warm her mother always felt.

"This is a happy day, Danielle." Mr. Fuller laid a

large, warm hand on her shoulder. "We knew the Lord had his eye on you, and it was only a matter of time till you set your eyes on him."

"Tell us about it, dear. How did it happen?"

Dani looked at her mother, knowing it wasn't necessary to burden her with the details that led to her commitment. Dredging up the hurts of the past summer wouldn't help anyone. She didn't want to worry her parents about that horrifying experience with Ken Bridges. "Edna was a real witness to me this summer. But as I was returning to San Francisco, I stopped at a little church in Mariposa. The pastor and his wife were so kind to me. They prayed with me, and even invited me to stay in their home for two days."

As Dani thought about the Fishers, she decided that early the next morning, she would call to assure them she was all right.

"I was praying that a change of setting would bring you around, Dani." Mrs. Fuller smiled. "The Lord knew right where to put you this summer."

"Amen," Mr. Fuller said.

"Honey, what happened to that Mrs. Talbott you were caring for?" her mother asked. "I never did understand how that fit in with your position at the publishing company."

"It was kind of a research job, Mom. It didn't turn out to be what was expected." Dani paused, her face strained. "And Edna, well, she had another heart attack. I called the hospital in Merced yesterday, and she's being transferred to Sacramento tomorrow." She looked at both of her folks. "Maybe we can visit her up there. You'd love her, she's a beautiful Christian."

The rest of the day, Dani relaxed on the patio in the chaise lounge. She had found a book about conservation on her father's bookshelf and immediately sat down to read it. She had grown to love the wilderness and the way she felt when in the mountains or at the seashore. A quotation by John Muir, the naturalist, reminded her of the words Josh had spoken on their last meeting. "Climb the mountains and get their good tidings. Nature's peace will flow into you as sunshine flows into trees. The winds will blow their own freshness into you and the storms their energy, while cares will drop off like autumn leaves."

"God's peace," Josh had said. Dani was glad she had found it. Dani let the book close and leaned her head back and shut her eyes. She could visualize herself standing on a high precipice overlooking a great valley churning with life. Roaring streams, cascading waterfalls, giant trees. She saw herself in a ranger's uniform as a guardian of the wilderness. Why not? She could go back to school and pick up the subjects she needed for a new career. The projected picture remained on the screen of her imagination, but it changed. No longer alone, she sensed a strong masculine presence beside her. Josh?

Her eyes flew open, the book slid from her lap to the ground. She was alone.

Only the clatter of pots and pans, and the aroma of Mom's favorite spice cake came through the open window of the kitchen. She was preparing a coming-home feast for her prodigal daughter. Yes, she was home. Home where it was safe. She'd think later about pursuing a forestry career. Right now, the remembrance of the men and women in green was too painful. Maybe in a few weeks. Maybe.

The days of the following week dragged by as Dani moped about the house trying to fit into a lifestyle she wasn't familiar with. Her parents seemed concerned and puzzled that she was so depressed, and she tried

161

to lighten her mood by listening to music and inviting her dad to join her on long walks through the countryside. But nothing helped. She was in limbo, not knowing where to turn. Her prayers seemed to bounce off the ceiling of her room, and the words of the Bible, which had previously been such a comfort, now blurred together without meaning.

"Honey, why don't you get away for the day?" her mother asked one morning over breakfast. "I know our days are quite boring to you, especially after living in San Francisco and traveling about so much."

She reached over to pat Dani's hand. "You seem so troubled, dear. I can't help but worry. Is there anything you want to tell me, any way I can help?"

The soft blue eyes crinkled at the corners, and Dani thought her mother had become more beautiful each year. She didn't want to be a burden to her, and knew she must make a move. The sooner the better.

Dani smiled brightly. "I think I do need to take a ride, Mom. Would you and Dad like to come along? I think I'll drive up to Grass Valley. I always liked it up there . . . might even be a little fall color by now." Already she felt better. She needed to get her mind off herself and the remorse she still felt about her deception to the Talbotts.

Just the thought of getting away for a day brought the color into her face and a sparkle to her eyes. Her father noticed the change as she strode through the living room. "Say, now there's our girl. Out for the day, huh?"

Dani perched herself on the arm of his chair and hugged him. "Thanks for everything, Dad. I know I've been moping around this past week. Just a lot of garbage to clean up, I guess."

"The Lord wants to carry all of your burdens, honey. Why don't you give it over to him?"

"I thought I did," she sighed. "That night in Mariposa, I prayed about everything."

162

"Well, I don't know what's bothering you, and if you don't want to talk about it, that's fine, but," he said, twisting a long curl that swept over her shoulder between his fingers, "sometimes, we can't really have the peace and blessing of God on our lives until we make things right with people, too."

That was it! She had known it in her heart, but hadn't wanted to face it. She would have to confess her deception to both Josh and Edna. Of course, he already knew she wasn't a nurse, but did he also know that she had come into his home to spy on him?

Dani nodded as she left the room. "You're right, Dad. I do need to see some people. Thanks."

Driving up the highway toward Sacramento, she assured herself that Amanda had probably already told Josh about Westcoast Publishing Company, and she may have even told Edna, but she wanted them both to know that her love for Edna was genuine and she hadn't betrayed any of their confidences.

She turned off Interstate 5 to Highway 80, planning to follow it up to Grass Valley, but when she reached the J-Street turnoff, her car automatically sped down the offramp. Mercy Hospital was only a short distance away, and she had to see how Edna had survived the surgery. She had prayed for her, and felt confident that God heard those prayers, at least.

Inside, the receptionist directed her to the cardiac care unit on the third floor, instructing her to stop off at the waiting room to call for permission to visit the patient. As Dani looked around the small anteroom, her heart ached for those awaiting word of their loved ones. Tired and disheveled, men and women slouched in chairs and on couches, probably having been there all night.

At last, a nurse appeared to direct her to Edna's room with the words, "She's still sedated from the

163

surgery yesterday, and won't know you're in the room. But she went through the procedure well and should be up walking in only a few days."

Dani felt like singing. Edna would be well again. How happy Josh must be.

"I think I should warn you," the nurse said before opening Edna's door, "heart surgery patients look terrible. She's still on the heart-lung machine, as well as many other tubes. Her skin is white and puffy, and all in all, you'd better get a good grip on yourself before going in."

Dani assured her that she would be fine, but when she stepped into the room, her head began to spin and her ears started to ring. Cold water filled her kneecaps and hot water rose in her throat. The nurse slipped an arm about her waist and led her out of the room and to a chair. "I warned you," she said, smiling.

"I guess I didn't take you seriously." She felt foolish, but added quickly, "You're sure she's going to be okay?"

"Positive. You come back tomorrow or the next day, and you won't believe this is the same woman!"

The nurse's hand was on Dani's elbow raising her to her feet when Josh stepped up to her.

"Dani!" His eyes searched her face. "I'm surprised to see you. I thought you'd dropped out of our lives for good." His tone was formal, but she caught a spark of pleasure in his voice.

"The nurse says she'll be all right," she said, motioning toward the room. "I'm afraid her appearance caught me off guard." She folded her hands tightly together to keep them from trembling. "I couldn't forget her Josh . . . ever."

"Dani, please wait for me. We need to talk."

Dani wished she had driven straight to Grass Valley, but she nodded obediently and walked down the hall in a daze.

This was her chance to confess her real purpose in going to Yosemite, and although she dreaded his reaction, she had to tell him. At least, she would have the past settled, and God would be able to guide her into the next phase of her life.

She had only waited in the hall a few minutes when she heard his footsteps echo down the corridor. A smile curved his lips, and his eyes, clear and bright, crinkled at the corners.

"Praise the Lord," he said in a reverent tone. "She's going to make it."

Dani weighed his comment over in her mind. She had never before heard him speak that way, but before she could comment, he asked, "How about some lunch?"

They decided to meet in Old Sacramento around noon after Josh had taken care of some hospital paperwork. Dani was relieved for the extra time she could use to decide how to tell him about her job and Westcoast Publishing Company. Maybe she would even tell him about her new commitment to Christ.

Old Sacramento had changed since her last visit. More buildings had been restored, and a highlight was the Railroad Museum. There was no time to go through it today, so she satisfied herself with browsing through a few gift shops. She tried to formulate in her mind how and when she would drop her bombshell. "Josh," she would say with a reserved air, "I'm not who you think I am. I came to Yosemite as a spy."

"Oh, here you are," Josh said over her shoulder. "Sorry I'm late. I've been making arrangements for Mother to be transferred to a convalescent home after she leaves the hospital. She'll only have to stay about a month, then she can move back to her own place." He smiled down at her. "Hungry?"

"Starved!" Dani glanced down at her clothes. She

had dressed for a day in the hills—jeans, bulky blue sweater, and tennis shoes. "Let's make it someplace casual, though. I was on my way to Grass Valley." She trotted along beside him, trying to keep up with his long strides. "Thought it would be nice up there—quiet and alone."

"You can find that in Yosemite, too," he replied, stepping up to a small café that offered old-fashioned service. "It's getting harder and harder to be alone, though. We had more visitors this year than ever before."

Josh held a chair while she sat down, then picked up a menu. "I'm asking for a transfer."

She felt her pulse quicken. "You're leaving Yosemite?" He and Amanda must be moving back to Washington or to some place that suited her better.

"Not right away, probably within the year though."

Dani changed the subject by asking about Betty, and Josh quickly brightened. "She's getting along fine," he said, puffing out his cheeks. "Adding a little weight, and happy as a kid at Christmas. Hard to imagine Betty and Bill as parents, they've been a couple for so long." He glanced over her head, then back into her eyes. "They're not taking parenthood lightly. In fact, they've both been praying about this for several years. According to Betty, at one time she had some physical problems that could have prevented her from ever getting pregnant. They were quite disappointed because they wanted a child so badly. But they just kept praying, and *voila*—a baby is on the way!"

Josh laughed and added, "They'll do great. I've made them promise to make me the godfather."

"You'd be a good father, too, Josh." Dani touched her fingers to her lips. Why had she said that?

"Yes, I think I would. I like kids. In fact, I'm taking a group of boys from the county home to the High

166

Country. Some of these kids have never been farther from home—if you can call what they live in a home—than their own crowded city streets. "Yes," he said, leaning forward in his chair, "I think I'd make some kid a good dad. How about you, Dani? Would you like to be a mother?"

Feeling her face flush, she sipped ice water and watched Josh over the edge of her glass. If only she hadn't stopped at the hospital, she wouldn't be here sitting so close to him, hearing his voice, sensing his vitality and warmth. If only . . . She suddenly realized she was staring and quickly lowered her eyes.

"Well, would you?"

"Would I what?"

"I asked if you would like to be a mother?"

Dani circled the rim of her glass with a forefinger, stalling for time. "I guess I've never given motherhood much thought. I used to do quite a bit of babysitting when I was a teenager and found little kids a lot of fun. I even took care of my cousin's new baby overnight several times." She paused, glancing up at Josh. "I don't like the crying or the late-night feedings, but I do love the challenge of teaching children."

"Yeah, kids can teach us a few things, too!"

"That's what Mom used to say. She said I was a living object lesson for her and that she learned about herself from me." Dani smiled across the table. "I have great parents. If I could be the kind of mother I had, then I'd say, 'Yes, I would like to be a mother.' Some day."

"Well, maybe you will be," Josh said, biting into his hamburger. "By the way, have you and Hutchinson set a date?" He folded his arms in front of him and looked her over. "He seems like a nice guy, not really your type, but then I'm not sure I know what type you prefer."

The bite of hamburger in her mouth seemed to swell, and she wondered if she could swallow it. Finally, after another drink of water, she answered, "I'm not sure, either, Josh." She tried to sound flippant. "But I guess you're as confused as I am. Have you set a date?"

"I asked first. You didn't answer my question."

"I can't imagine where you got the idea that Mark and I were serious."

"Well, you did spend the night in his room at the Ahwahnee, didn't you?"

"I was in the room alone, if you must know. Mark left that night."

A smile emphasized the creases in his cheeks and his mustache quivered. "I know. I saw him leave, and was he mad!" He chuckled, his eyes never leaving hers.

"What do you mean 'you saw'? You were following me?"

"In a way." He paused. "I didn't want you to be smooth-talked by that city dude."

"So that's why you weren't home all night. You were spying on me!" Her words came in short spurts. "Of all the nerve, accusing me of . . . when you knew I was innocent. Do you think I need you to watch over me? Well, I don't. I don't need you or your false conclusions or anything else!"

Dani stood up. "I'll try to keep in touch with Edna, but as for you, I'd appreciate it if you and your precious Amanda would stay out of my life."

Eyes about to overflow with tears, she dashed through the door of the café. It seemed she was always making a dramatic exit. No more. This was it. Finis!

CHAPTER 12

THE MONTH OF SEPTEMBER had come and gone with Dani only going through the motions of living. She had kept track of Edna's progress by telephone, and was confident that by now her friend's health was much improved. The desire to go to Sacramento to visit Edna tugged at her heart, but she didn't want to have another confrontation with Josh.

Josh had called several times. Dani had refused to come to the phone and her father said Josh wouldn't leave a message.

Dani did all in her power to forget him. She drove to Stockton twice a week for a biology class at the community college, and had decided to pick up the subjects she needed there, then transfer to Santa Rosa Junior College where a course was available for prospective rangers. At least it was something to plan for.

"Honey, I don't see how you keep so busy," her mother said one morning. "All that study and working at the church three days a week. Aren't you overdoing it?"

"I have to make some money, Mom." She smiled up from her books. "Can't leech off you the rest of my life."

"How about your savings? You said you had some put away."

"I'll need that when I transfer to Santa Rosa, and I want to help out here as much as I can."

"Well, I do wish you'd get out with some young people your age. You shouldn't stick so close to home." Her mother frowned, then added, "Aren't there any men in the church that interest you? How about that Brad fellow?"

"Mom, come here." Dani motioned toward the bed and watched her mother sit down. "I haven't talked to you about the past because I felt I'd been enough trouble to you and Dad, but . . ." She breathed deeply. "I do want to tell you something. I . . . I fell in love while I was in Yosemite."

She smiled. Somehow it eased the pain to talk about it. "Joshua Talbott was all I ever wanted in a man. We like the same music and authors. He's honest and forthright and genuinely cares about people. He's got a good sense of humor and he's a Christian. Besides all that," she added, her eyes sparkling and her dimple sinking in deeply as she smiled, "he's the most handsome, romantic man in the whole world!"

Gladys Fuller grinned as she watched her daughter. "Well, then, why on earth did you come home? What happened?"

"He's married."

"Oh! Dani, you should have never allowed yourself to think of him in that way."

"He wasn't married then, Mom." She paused and wiped at a tear. "But I'm sure he is now."

"Is he the one who's been calling you?"

"Yes, and I don't know why. I keep in touch about Edna's condition." She inhaled as if drawing her last breath. "I just can't talk to him about the way I feel. I've already made such a fool of myself over him. I'm just hoping my misery will pass."

"I've been praying for you, honey. I could see how unhappy you are. I wish you'd told me about this sooner."

"I couldn't talk about it before, but somehow it doesn't hurt quite as much now. Maybe I'm getting over him."

"Well, I certainly hope so." Mrs. Fuller started to get up, then asked, "How about that Mr. Hutchinson? Didn't you talk to him a few times when you first came home?"

"It was just business." She shrugged. "I thought at one time I was interested in Mark, but that was before I met Josh."

As her mother started to leave, Dani asked, "Can you ever get over loving someone?"

"With God all things are possible," her mother quoted. "If Joshua Talbott is married, it's obvious he's not God's choice for you, isn't it?" She stepped over to Dani and cradled her head in her arms. "You gave the Lord your life, honey. Let him heal your pain and put it all back together."

Dani looked up into the soft blue eyes. She was right. If there was another man for her, the Lord would bring him along at the right time. Until then, she would devote herself to her studies and her part-time job.

A sense of peace filled her heart as she returned to her books. She only wanted the best for Josh, too. He belonged to the Lord, and she had to trust him to guide both their lives.

That afternoon as Dani sorted through the mail, she found a letter addressed to her in a woman's handwriting. The return address was Yosemite. Betty! How wonderful to hear from her.

Dani ripped open the envelope and curled up in a big wicker chair on the front porch. It already felt like fall—the air was warm with a touch of crispness, and that lazy contentment that she always experienced this time of year was upon her. She gave her attention to the letter. After a brief greeting, Betty wrote,

Bill and I are awfully disappointed, but we're keeping our eyes on the Lord. We thought it was his time for us to have a child, but I lost it last week. We don't understand what we're to learn through this, but our heartache has driven us closer to God and to each other.

Dani felt the tears begin to well up in her eyes, and looked out across the fields that surrounded the small house. She could almost feel the emptiness that Betty wrote about.

Josh has been such a comfort to us, too. I knew that once he committed himself to Christ, he'd be a firebrand. He's taken a group of high school boys from our church to the high country on backpacking trips, and may even recruit some future men for the National Park Service as well as for Christ!

We're really going to miss him. I was sorry to hear that his transfer came through so quickly. Well, I'll close now. I'm not feeling great yet, and my mind kind of wanders. Just wanted to let you know what's happening up here. Miss you.

> Love,
> Betty

Dani folded the letter and bowed her head. "Oh, Lord, I'm so sorry for them. Please give them your strength . . . and another baby. They'd make such good parents."

What was it she'd said about Josh? Dani opened the letter and reread it. Nothing had been said about

Amanda or the wedding. Nothing at all. Betty had written of Josh's walk with the Lord and his interest in young people. Then she had hinted about his transfer. His transfer? Amanda's influence no doubt. Was it the desk job she wanted him to have? Was he giving up his fieldwork? Dani had to know.

With her heart pounding, she ran to the telephone and dialed the Talbotts' number. No answer. She flipped through her address book but she didn't have Betty's telephone number. Park Headquarters. She'd call them. Once again she dialed, hoping that Josh was there so she could hear his voice. She would just ask about Betty, of course.

"Yosemite National Park. Erma speaking."

"Erma, this is Danielle Fuller. Is Joshua Talbott in?"

"No, he's not. He and Mrs. Talbott are no longer here."

"You mean," Dani said, clearing her throat, "he's not working at Yosemite anymore?"

"That's right. I believe he's on a leave right now. He's in the process of moving." She paused, waiting for a response. "Would you like to speak to someone else?"

"No, thank you." Dani replaced the receiver and slumped her shoulders. He and *Mrs.* Talbott were gone. It was over. He had probably transferred to an area where Amanda could continue her psychiatric treatment. Dani's heart ached with a pain that traveled through her shoulders and to her fingertips. She couldn't imagine Yosemite Valley without Josh. Her eyes brightened, she could see Betty without the worry of running into him.

"Mom!" Dani ran into the kitchen. "I think I'll take a trip up to Yosemite. I just got a letter," she said, waving it in the air, "from a friend of mine who lost her baby. I think I could be an encouragement to her."

All smiles, her mother said, "I know you could. And it would be good for you, too. The mountains are beautiful this time of year." She paused, biting at her lower lip. "But be careful, the weather forecast predicted a storm on the way."

With her mind set on leaving early the next morning, Dani called the church office to let them know, and made reservations at Yosemite Lodge for the next three nights. That would give her a couple of days with Betty without missing any classes and only one day of work. Her face glowed as she packed her clothes, and she noticed both her mother and father smiled at each other with pleasure.

"You guys don't have to be so happy that I'm leaving," she teased. "I'm coming back, you know."

"We're just happy to see you looking forward to something."

"I guess I have been droopy lately," she said, hugging them both. "I couldn't have made it without you and the Lord!"

After saying good-night, she fell into a deep sleep, content with the thought that even if she didn't see Josh, she would have a couple of glorious days in his "Incomparable Valley."

The trip to the High Sierra passed without incident. She hovered between the decision to stop in Mariposa to see the Fishers or not, then decided she could drop in on her way back home. She wanted to get to Yosemite as soon as possible. The time with Betty would be healing for both of them.

The sheer walls of the valley surrounded her with a fresh sense of God's presence. It was much stronger than she had remembered, but then so was her faith. Leaves in various shades of orange and yellow drifted lazily to the ground with each puff of breeze. The ground cover of ferns wore a golden hue now, and would soon be clothed with the first snow of the season. Maybe sooner than she hoped if the weatherman was right about that approaching storm.

After checking into the lodge, she drove up the familiar road to the rangers' homes, hoping Betty would be glad to see her.

But without a pause, she drove past Betty's house and stopped in front of the Talbotts'. The familiar park truck was gone. It looked empty, deserted. One last peek in the window would put this part of her life behind her.

As she neared the front porch, she could see the furniture still rested in its original places. Josh hadn't moved yet. But where was he? She pressed her nose against the window and peered in. Some of the things were gone, but most of the pieces were still there. As a little circle of steam formed around her mouth, blocking her vision, she realized how cool the day had become and thought of her jacket in the trunk of the car. No time for that now. She fumbled in her purse for the key to the Talbotts' home. She would go in and leave it on the kitchen counter for the next chief ranger.

Inside, the house felt cold and lonely. She glanced down the hall where she had last followed the gurney to the ambulance. So much had happened in the past six weeks. How lonely and empty the living room was without Edna and Josh. In fact, many things were not the same. The costly pieces of china were gone. Amanda probably saw to it that they were the first things moved. The Oriental rugs had been removed, too, revealing only the shining oak floors. A few tables were missing, and most of the sculpture. Amanda must have stalked the movers to see that they were packed first.

Dani whistled to herself to break the silence and sauntered down the hall, first peeking into Edna's room, then the one that had been hers. She knew

Edna's personal belongings had been shipped to her apartment in Sacramento, but most of the furniture was in place. Looking at the rocking chair where Edna had sat to read the Bible brought tears to her eyes. What sweet moments they had spent together.

In the kitchen, she opened the cupboard and smiled at the memory of Josh reaching for china plates and crystal goblets for their midnight snack of eggs and milk. They had talked so freely then. Reluctantly, she laid her house key on the kitchen table.

She flipped her hair behind her shoulders and ventured back down the hall. Was Josh's room the same? Did he still have the waterbed? Had Amanda slept in it? A sinking sensation crept over her as she looked up the stairs. Could she go into that room again, knowing Amanda had been there as Josh's wife?

Yes. Dani plodded up the steps one at a time, dreading, yet somehow anticipating seeing that room once more. As before, the drapes were drawn, and she groped around in the dark until her eyes became accustomed to the dimness. The stereo was still in the corner, with tapes scattered about. Why hadn't he done more packing? If he had already been transferred, perhaps movers were coming in to do all the packing.

Walking to the closet, she snapped on the switch before opening the door. No women's clothes! Where were Amanda's things? And all those beautiful clothes that had been Marlena's?

Dani's heart fluttered as the spicy, leathery fragrance she associated with Josh filled her senses. She lifted the sleeve of his tweed jacket and buried her face in its rough texture. She pushed it back into the closet. Why was she torturing herself like this?

She continued to look around the room for signs of Amanda's presence, but there were none. No smells of perfume, no feminine touches at all. Strange.

176

Suddenly she became aware of movement and glanced toward the bed. A big lump moved, causing the bed to sway. She clutched her heart and held her breath. Someone was asleep in Josh's bed! Waiting until the person once again breathed slowly and rhythmically, she tiptoed closer and leaned over.

Josh! He should have been in another national park miles away from here.

Knowing she must get away before he awoke, she carefully made her way to the stairs, but as she started down, she bumped against a small table and rattled a lamp.

"Who's there?" Josh mumbled.

Dani didn't wait for another word, but sprinted down the steps and out the front door. No time to see Betty now. She leaped into her car and sped down the hill, her heart pounding in her ears. She didn't know why he was still here, but she knew he would be terribly angry if he caught her snooping yet again.

Dani lifted her foot off the accelerator as she neared the Yosemite Falls parking area. A walk to the top of the falls was something she had attempted once—the night of Amanda's arrival—why not give it another try? She could work off her nervous energy. She swung the small car into a parking space, and was on her way up the path before she could think twice. Her trusty jogging shoes wouldn't let her down, but she probably should have brought along her jacket. With her heart still racing with the excitement of hearing Josh's voice, she proceeded to climb with ease.

After hiking for about a half hour, she stopped to catch her breath, and decided not to go see Betty after all. She would stay at the lodge overnight, then return to Lodi in the morning. With that settled, she resumed her climb, a little surprised that there was no one else on the trail.

Onward and upward she climbed, noticing along the

177

way that parts of the path had crumbled and fallen off. She remembered Josh speaking about sections of the trail that needed repair, but it was surely safe or there would be signs posted.

Dani edged her way around boulders, holding tightly to sharp rocks and protruding twigs. She leaned against the black granite and breathed deeply. The cold air hurt her lungs. The climb had been harder than she had anticipated and she was tiring, but believing the crest to be about a hundred yards ahead, she continued on.

"Oh," she shrieked when a portion of the path crumbled off behind her. Dirt and rocks clattered down the cliff. It left only a very narrow piece of ground on which to cross. She hoped she wouldn't have trouble getting back down. Not wanting to think about anything but reaching the top, she pressed on.

Cold and shaking now, she felt like kicking herself for not bringing her coat. How foolish. How foolish she had been to run from Josh when she longed so desperately to see him.

As she stood at the side of the mountain, a fine mist dusted her face, but it wasn't from the falls. It was too cold for that. The storm was on the way, and she was on top of a mountain without a coat! She must get back to her car. Posthaste! Before dark. She could never find her way down at night without slipping and falling to her death. *Oh, Lord, I need you. I've really gotten myself into a mess this time!*

As Dani began her descent, heavy black clouds swept over the valley, bringing a cold wind that slapped against her face and clawed at her clothes. Her feet slipped and slid over wet rocks and crumbling earth, and her hands bled from grasping at the sharp boulders to keep from falling. She was trapped.

The path had dropped away, and there was no way down the side of the mountain. Panic gripped her. She would die here. She would freeze to death and plunge over the waterfall, undiscovered until the spring thaw. Hot tears mingled with cold flakes for only an instant before the wind whipped them away.

Fear thou not; for I am with thee: be not dismayed; for I am thy God: I will strengthen thee; yea, I will help thee; yea, I will uphold thee with the right hand of my righteousness. A long forgotten memory verse calmed her heart. God's promise to care for her banished the fear that had gripped her. He would help, and with his hand he would keep her feet on the path.

As her senses cleared, she began to look around for a way to keep warm and dry until morning. By then, someone would have seen her car and come looking for her.

She edged her way back up the path, feeling along the rocks for a crevice where she might find shelter. A hymn she had sung as a child played in her mind, *The Lord's our Rock, in him we hide, a shelter in the time of storm.*

Although the sky was darker now, and the crack barely visible, Dani found a large crevice, almost a cave, beside the path. She stooped down and crawled inside. It seemed to be about six feet deep, two or three feet wide, and high enough for her to sit comfortably. Straining her eyes, she was glad to discover that other than a soft layer of moss, she was the only living thing in the cave.

She pulled the collar of her shirt as high around her neck as she could and curled up into a ball. "Lord, I know that you are right here with me," she prayed, "and it's such a comfort. I know there's a possibility that I might see you face-to-face tonight, and if I do, please help those who love me not to be too sad. But," she added, her voice rising loud enough for her to hear above the wind outside, "if you have some more living for me to do, then I'd sure be glad to see a rescuer!"

A shrill whistling awakened Dani from a fitful sleep, and she wrapped her arms around her knees and drew them closer to her chest, trying to close out the fierce wind that gusted and ripped around the entrance of her small haven. Although she was protected from the elements, occasional flakes of snow drifted through the opening, bringing dampness and cold. It would be impossible for someone to reach her tonight. Maybe even impossible tomorrow. What were those words her mother had said? "With God nothing is impossible!"

With that thought, she fell into a deep sleep.

"Dani! Dani! Where are you? If you can hear me, please answer!"

An anguished voice called her name. Or was she only dreaming it? She lifted her head. So tired. So cold.

"Dani!" The voice was nearer. Someone had come for her. But she was so sleepy. Maybe they would come back another day. She closed her eyes and drifted . . . drifted.

"Dani! Answer me! Can you hear me?"

She opened her eyes again. "Is that you, Josh?" she whispered.

"Dani!" The voice was right outside her little cave now. She tried to answer, but no sound came from her lips. She touched them. They were so cold. So were her fingers. Cold. Everything was cold.

"Please answer me." The voice had passed her. She must stop him. If he went much farther, he would slip off the path. It was narrower and more dangerous up ahead.

She forced herself to a crawling position. The skin on her knees and palms felt like tissue paper stretched over blocks of ice. If she moved too quickly, they would surely rip open. With excruciating pain, she crawled to the entrance and poked out her head. A blast of icy wind whipped her face.

"Josh!" The wind carried her voice back down the mountain. She could barely see a form on the path ahead. She must stop him. "Josh!" she called, surprised at the sudden strength of her vocal chords. The figure turned.

"Dani!" He moved slowly toward her, feeling his way along the dark path. "Thank God. You're alive!"

Dani backed into the cave as he knelt down and squeezed into the small opening. "Thank God!" he said again.

Without another word, he opened his down jacket and drew her inside next to his warm body. "Oh, Dani, I found you. I found you."

She felt his tears fall onto her face, warm and sweet. She wanted to speak, but was so cold and numb.

"Here, let me warm you. It's a miracle you didn't freeze to death."

He stretched out beside her and wrapped her up in his jacket. She was trembling now, whether from the cold or the exhilaration, she didn't know. Like an answer to her prayer, a rescuer had come. Josh was beside her, his arms around her, his chin resting on her head. Next to her cheek, his heart pounded, warming his blood and hers as she nestled in his arms. Neither of them spoke as they lay in the darkness. There was nothing she could say. She was only thankful to be warm again. To be alive.

In spite of herself, she kept slipping off to sleep, then awaking in a start to find she was still enclosed in the warm embrace of the only man she would ever love.

"Josh?" She lifted her face to his. "Thank you for coming after me. I had no idea the path was so bad, or that it would storm." She shivered again. "I'm sorry I've been so much trouble to you."

She lay very still waiting for his answer, but his arms only held her tighter.

After several minutes, she seemed to be warmer and her mind cleared. "I shouldn't have come up here—to Yosemite—I mean. I was going to see Betty, but . . . ," she said, pausing. "I just had to see the house once more."

Josh's lips moved in her hair, his warm breath sending thrills through her body. "I know," he said at last. "I saw you in my room." He chuckled. "You do love to come up there, don't you?"

"I had to see . . . I . . . ," she stammered, "I had to know about Amanda and you."

"Amanda and me?" He buried his face in her hair. "I thought someone had told you. She's gone, and taken all the memories of the past with her. I finally realized what a manipulator she was." He stroked her hair, then pressed her head against his chest. "I've tried to tell you several times, but you always managed to get away before I could explain." A soft laugh rippled in his throat. "Remember the day she went to tell Mother you weren't a nurse?"

Dani's head bobbed up and down under his chin.

"Well, that day, it all came out about her involvement with some Ken Bridges character and a book he planned to write. He worked for Mark Hutchinson, learned about Marlena's death, and contacted Amanda."

Dani shuddered, and Josh held her closer.

"It seems their scheme also involved swindling me out of Marlena's inheritance, and in the process, disparaging me with the National Park Service. I guess Amanda's purpose was revenge, and Bridges' was greed. Your friend Mark Hutchinson clued me in on Bridges' part of the scheme, and the whole ugly mess came to light just after Mother's surgery.''

Dani felt her mind must still be numb with cold. It all seemed so fantastic. Why hadn't Mark told her about all of this? If he couldn't have her, he didn't want Josh to, either. That's the only way she could explain his actions.

"Anyway," he said, tipping her face to his, "that's what I've been trying to tell you for a month, but I finally decided you meant it when you said you didn't want to see me ever again."

"Oh, Josh, I didn't mean it.'' She couldn't see his face in the darkness, but his nearness overwhelmed her. "I wanted so badly to tell you about my job with Westcoast, and something always stopped me."

She wrapped her arms around his waist, enjoying the warmth returning to every part of her body. "I loved you so much, I couldn't bear to think of you with Amanda. I thought you two were already married. I've been so miserable."

"So have I, my darling," he cooed. "So have I."

With one arm still around her back, he stroked her hair away from her face and touched his lips to her brow. "I'll never let you go again. In fact," he said, kissing the tip of her nose, "as soon as we get out of here in the morning, you and I are driving to Lodi to ask your father's permission to marry!"

"Oh," she said, pretending to be offended. "Don't you think you should ask my permission first?" She turned her face away from his kisses. "Maybe I'm not ready for marriage."

He held her closer, his lips whispering over her eyes, her cheeks, and as she lifted her face, their lips met gently at first; then as they gave in to their love, their kisses were passionate, hungry. Finally, she pulled away and drew a deep breath. "On second thought, I think I am ready!"

"I can't live without you, Danielle Fuller. You've invaded my valley, my home, my heart. I was so miserable when I thought you'd never come back, but the Lord has used this time to help me mature. Since Christ has become Lord of my life, I know for certain that he has kept you for me. Please be my wife, my darling. Please come back with me."

Her heart was so full of love, she could hardly speak. "Josh, I'll go anywhere you go, you know that! I've always loved you. I always will." She paused. "But where are we going? Where have you been transferred?"

"I asked for a cancellation today. I thought I wanted to get away from here—Mirror Lake, the falls, you were everywhere. It meant nothing to me without you, but I needed some memories of that blonde who had invaded my life so I asked to stay."

With his forefinger, he traced the outline of her face, beginning at her forehead, over her nose, her lips, her chin. "Will you be happy here?"

"In your 'Incomparable Valley'? It's where I found love, where I found . . ."

But Dani didn't finish her sentence, because Josh's warm lips covered hers, closing out all other thoughts.

ABOUT THE AUTHOR

A homemaker and freelance writer, SHIRLEY COOK has been writing for publication for more than a decade. She's the author of six books, including *The Marriage Puzzle*, and numerous magazine articles.

Cook's no stranger to Yosemite National Park, in which *Through the Valley of Love* is set. She and her husband of thirty-six years live in California's San Joaquin Valley and have six grown children.

A Letter to Our Readers

Dear Reader:

Welcome to Serenade Books—a series designed to bring you beautiful love stories in the world of inspirational romance. They will uplift you, encourage you, and provide hours of wholesome entertainment, so thousands of readers have testified. That we might better contribute to your reading enjoyment, we would appreciate your taking a few minutes to respond to the following questions and return to:

> Lois Taylor
> Serenade Books
> The Zondervan Publishing House
> 1415 Lake Drive, S.E.
> Grand Rapids, Michigan 49506

1. Did you enjoy reading *Through the Valley of Love*?

   ☐ Very much. I would like to see more books by this author!
   ☐ Moderately
   ☐ I would have enjoyed it more if _____

2. Where did you purchase this book? _____

3. What influenced your decision to purchase this book?

   ☐ Cover   ☐ Back cover copy
   ☐ Title   ☐ Friends
   ☐ Publicity   ☐ Other _____

4. Please rate the following elements from 1 (poor) to 10 (superior).

☐ Heroine   ☐ Plot
☐ Hero   ☐ Inspirational theme
☐ Setting   ☐ Secondary characters

5. What are some inspirational themes you would like to see treated in future books?

_____

_____

6. Please indicate your age range:

☐ Under 18   ☐ 25–34   ☐ 46–55
☐ 18–24   ☐ 35–45   ☐ Over 55

Serenade / Saga books are inspirational romances in historical settings, designed to bring you a joyful, heart-lifting reading experience.

Serenade / Saga books available in your local bookstore:

#1 *Summer Snow*, Sandy Dengler
#2 *Call Her Blessed*, Jeanette Gilge
#3 *Ina*, Karen Baker Kletzing
#4 *Juliana of Clover Hill*, Brenda Knight Graham
#5 *Song of the Nereids*, Sandy Dengler
#6 *Anna's Rocking Chair*, Elaine Watson
#7 *In Love's Own Time*, Susan C. Feldhake
#8 *Yankee Bride*, Jane Peart
#9 *Light of My Heart*, Kathleen Karr
#10 *Love Beyond Surrender*, Susan C. Feldhake
#11 *All the Days After Sunday*, Jeanette Gilge
#12 *Winterspring*, Sandy Dengler
#13 *Hand Me Down the Dawn*, Mary Harwell Sayler
#14 *Rebel Bride*, Jane Peart
#15 *Speak Softly, Love*, Kathleen Yapp
#16 *From This Day Forward*, Kathleen Karr
#17 *The River Between*, Jacquelyn Cook
#18 *Valiant Bride*, Jane Peart
#19 *Wait for the Sun*, Maryn Langer
#20 *Kincaid of Cripple Creek*, Peggy Darty
#21 *Love's Gentle Journey*, Kay Cornelius
#22 *Applegate Landing*, Jean Conrad
#23 *Beyond the Smoky Curtain*, Mary Harwell Sayler
#24 *To Dwell in the Land*, Elaine Watson
#25 *Moon for a Candle*, Maryn Langer
#26 *The Conviction of Charlotte Grey*, Jeanne Cheyney
#27 *Opal Fire*, Sandy Dengler
#28 *Divide the Joy*, Maryn Langer
#29 *Cimarron Sunset*, Peggy Darty

#30 *This Rolling Land*, Sandy Dengler
#31 *The Wind Along the River*, Jacquelyn Cook
#32 *Sycamore Settlement*, Suzanne Pierson Ellison
#33 *Where Morning Dawns*, Irene Brand
#34 *Elizabeth of Saginaw Bay*, Donna Winters
#35 *Westward My Love*, Elaine L. Schulte
#36 *Ransomed Bride*, Jane Peart
#37 *Dreams of Gold*, Elaine L. Schulte

Serenade / Serenata books are inspirational romances in contemporary settings, designed to bring you a joyful, heart-lifting reading experience.

Serenade / Serenata books available in your local bookstore:

#1 *On Wings of Love*, Elaine L. Schulte
#2 *Love's Sweet Promise*, Susan C. Feldhake
#3 *For Love Alone*, Susan C. Feldhake
#4 *Love's Late Spring*, Lydia Heermann
#5 *In Comes Love*, Mab Graff Hoover
#6 *Fountain of Love*, Velma S. Daniels and Peggy E. King
#7 *Morning Song*, Linda Herring
#8 *A Mountain to Stand Strong*, Peggy Darty
#9 *Love's Perfect Image*, Judy Baer
#10 *Smoky Mountain Sunrise*, Yvonne Lehman
#11 *Greengold Autumn*, Donna Fletcher Crow
#12 *Irresistible Love*, Elaine Anne McAvoy
#13 *Eternal Flame*, Lurlene McDaniel
#14 *Windsong*, Linda Herring
#15 *Forever Eden*, Barbara Bennett
#16 *Call of the Dove*, Madge Harrah
#17 *The Desires of Your Heart*, Donna Fletcher Crow
#18 *Tender Adversary*, Judy Baer
#19 *Halfway to Heaven*, Nancy Johanson
#20 *Hold Fast the Dream*, Lurlene McDaniel
#21 *The Disguise of Love*, Mary LaPietra
#22 *Through a Glass Darkly*, Sara Mitchell
#23 *More Than a Summer's Love*, Yvonne Lehman
#24 *Language of the Heart*, Jeanne Anders
#25 *One More River*, Suzanne Pierson Ellison
#26 *Journey Toward Tomorrow*, Karyn Carr
#27 *Flower of the Sea*, Amanda Clark
#28 *Shadows Along the Ice*, Judy Baer

#29 *Born to Be One*, Cathie LeNoir
#30 *Heart Aflame*, Susan Kirby
#31 *By Love Restored*, Nancy Johanson
#32 *Karaleen*, Mary Carpenter Reid
#33 *Love's Full Circle*, Lurlene McDaniel
#34 *A New Love*, Mab Graff Hoover
#35 *The Lessons of Love*, Susan Phillips
#36 *For Always*, Molly Noble Bull
#37 *A Song in the Night*, Sara Mitchell
#38 *Love Unmerited*, Donna Fletcher Crow
#39 *Thetis Island*, Brenda Willoughby
#40 *Love More Precious*, Marilyn Austin

Watch for other books in both the *Serenade/Saga* (historical) and *Serenade/Serenata* (contemporary) series, coming soon.